Disney California Adventure Details

Popsicle stick bench in A Bug's Land

Bulletin board in
Buena Vista Street

License plate honoring
Roy E. Disney
(Walt's nephew)
in Grizzly Peak

Sand dollar
speaker in
Paradise Pier

Inside Flo's
V8 Café
in Cars Land

Photo spot in
Pacific Wharf

An unusual tree in
Hollywood Land

"I'm sorry, but how can one possibly pay attention to a book with no pictures in it?"
—ALICE

Table of Contents

What are you going to bring?

The early days of Disney California Adventure

The park's 7 themed lands

Write down what YOU think!

Collect character autographs here!

Disney Dictionary

Here are some Disney words and phrases to know before you go:

A **ATTRACTION**—Things at the park to see, do or ride are called attractions. These can be anything from a drawing class to a live show to a roller coaster.

C **CAST MEMBER**—In a play or movie, the performers are called the cast. The people who work in the Disneyland Resort are performing their jobs for the resort's visitors, so they are called Cast Members.

D **DCA**—DCA is short for "Disney California Adventure." Many visitors call the park "DCA" or "California Adventure" rather than its whole name.

DISNEY LEGEND—People who have made an extraordinary contribution to The Walt Disney Company are named Disney Legends—a sort of Hall of Fame for Disney employees.

DISNEYLAND RESORT—When Disney California Adventure and Downtown Disney opened near Disneyland, the name of the entire area was changed to the Disneyland Resort.

G **GUEST**—Disney California Adventure calls its visitors Guests and loves to make them feel special. If you ever have to sign for something in the park, Cast Members will often ask for your autograph instead of your signature.

H **HIDDEN MICKEY**—A Hidden Mickey is where the shape of Mickey Mouse is hidden in attractions and other spots in the park. Hidden Mickeys are used as decorations on products for sale too. Sometimes Mickey's whole body is shown but usually it's the simple three-circle symbol that looks like Mickey's head.

I **IMAGINEER**—This term is a combination of the words "imagination" and "engineer." It describes the talented people who create the magic in Disney parks. They design and oversee every detail, from the machinery that will make a ride work right down to the pattern of the wallpaper inside a restaurant.

Special Stuff in This Book

Look out for these handy dandy symbols and features!

The **Hot Tip** symbol is found near insider info that not just everyone knows about.

Eye Spy symbols let you know about special things to spy with your little eye.

If you love to color, you may enjoy coloring in the **black-and-white images** in this book. Sharp colored pencils or colored ballpoint pens will work best.

SO YOU KNOW...
blah, blah, blah

These **So You Know** areas explain a little bit more about words or phrases you might not know, like "grotto," "venue," and "zephyr."

This **stamp** tells you what type of attraction it is, what year it opened in Disney California Adventure and what it's like. Slower attractions are "Calm & Mellow," faster attractions are "Wild & Thrilling" and the ones that are somewhere in between are "Lively & Exciting."

There's a **scrapbook** on pages 166–169. While you're in Disney California Adventure, save any tags, receipts, tickets and other flat things so you can add them to the scrapbook later.

The fun doesn't have to stop because you're standing in line. Play **Waiting Games** when you're waiting for a ride, sitting in a restaurant or just taking a break. Time flies when you're having fun.

The smiley **Fun Fact** symbol is found near extra tidbits of fun and fascinating trivia.

MAY BE SCARY

This **caution** sign near the name of an attraction means that some people find it scary. If you're unsure, ask a Cast Member what to expect.

★ ★ ★ ★ ★ ★ ★ ★ ★ ★ A WORD TO THE WISE ★ ★ ★ ★ ★ ★ ★ ★ ★ ★

There are lots of activities, games and fill-in-the-blank areas in this book. A ballpoint pen or pencil will work best. Don't use markers because the ink might bleed through to the other side of the page.

Hollywood Land's realistic backdrop recreates Hollywood's famous theaters and landmarks.

My Trip Planner

Use this handy Trip Planner to get ready for your visit to DCA!

My TRiP PLANNeR—ItineRARY

How excited are you about visiting DCA? Draw an arrow from the black circle below to the word that best describes how you feel:

SO YOU KNOW...
itinerary = detailed plan for a trip

eXCiTeD-o-MeTeR

PRETTY VERY

FAIRLY BEYOND

Date(s) of visit to Disney California Adventure: ....

How many days will you be there? ....

Who are you going with? ....

....

Will you be going to Disneyland? ☐ Yes ☐ No

Will you be staying in a hotel? ☐ Yes ☐ No

If yes, what's it called? ....

Write other interesting details about your trip plans here:

....

....

My Trip Planner—Packing List

What are you going to bring with you?

....

....

....

....

....

....

....

....

....

....

....

....

....

....

....

My TRiP PLanneR—aBOUT My PLans

NOTE: *Fill this page out **after** you've read this book.*

Which **ATTRACTIONS** do you want to do?

....

....

....

....

....

....

....

Do you want to ride King Triton's Carousel?
☐ Yes ☐ No

MY TRiP PLANNER—aBOUT MY PLANS

NOTE: Fill this page out *after* you've read this book.

Which **ENTERTAINMENT** do you want to see?

....

....

....

....

....

....

Which **FOOD & DRINKS** do you want to try?

....

....

....

....

....

....

....

My Trip Planner—about My Plans

*NOTE: Fill this page out **after** you've read this book.*

Which **CHARACTERS** do want to see?

....

....

....

....

....

....

Draw your favorite Disney character:

MY TRIP PLANNER—COUNTDOWN

How many days until you go to Disney California Adventure? . . . .

When it's exactly 10 days before your visit, start this countdown by coloring in the 10 circle. Each day, color in the next shape in the countdown until it's time for your trip. For days 10–2 use a black crayon (or colored pencil). For the last day, color in the bowtie with red to complete the picture.

Wahoo!
You're going to Disney California Adventure!

GOING TO DISNEY
CALIFORNIA ADVENTURE
❧ **OFFICIAL FAN CLUB MEMBER** ☙

This card hereby certifies that:

_____

_____ is a fan of Going To Disney California Adventure

This member is a: ☐ Princess ☐ Prince ☐ Villain

☐ Other _____

Member Since: _____

Going To Guides
PO Box 217
Lafayette, CA 94549
www.GoingToGuides.com

Going To Guides — APPROVED BY Slasky — Going to DCA

GOING TO
DISNEYLAND
❧ **OFFICIAL FAN CLUB MEMBER** ☙

This card hereby certifies that:

_____

_____ is a fan of Going To Disneyland!

This member is a: ☐ Princess ☐ Prince ☐ Villain

☐ Other _____

Member Since: _____

Going To Guides
PO Box 217
Lafayette, CA 94549
www.GoingToGuides.com

Going To Guides — APPROVED BY Slasky — Going to Disneyland

Would YOU like to be in the Fan Club?

Fill out the cards above and you're in the club!
If you'd like to get actual cards or other fun goodies
like bookmarks, buttons, gift tags and stickers
—all made from art in the Going To Guides books—
visit the "GoingToGuides" shop on Etsy:
www.etsy.com/shop/goingtoguides
If you share pix of you with your goodies or book
on Instagram, Facebook or Twitter, be sure to
tag @GoingToGuides so we can see too!

GOING TO GUIDES

Disney's California

What Will You Find in This Chapter?

California Dreaming

Disney California Adventure—or DCA—is a sunny celebration of the Golden State of California. This fabulously fun theme park sits right across from Disneyland—Disney's first theme park ever in the whole wide world. These two parks are part of the Disneyland Resort but it wasn't always this way...

★ Destination Vacation

When you go to the Disneyland Resort today, you soon realize there's no way you could do everything in one visit. But back when Disneyland opened, there was only Disneyland and the Disneyland Hotel. Many Guests experienced the park in one day and went on their way. Years later, out in Florida, Disney fans were enjoying the Walt Disney World Resort where they could visit multiple Disney parks, explore a shopping area and stay at one of several Disney hotels. The Walt Disney Company wanted a similar experience for their California Guests so, in the 1990s, plans were made to create a second theme park somewhere near Disneyland.

TIME MACHINE

1955
Disneyland opens on July 17th & the Disneyland Hotel welcomes its first Guests three months later.

1991
The Walt Disney Company announces plans to build a new park across from Disneyland.

1995
Disney buys an existing hotel & five years later renames it Paradise Pier Hotel after the land in DCA that it will overlook.

2001
Disney's Grand Californian Hotel & Spa & Downtown Disney open a month before DCA in January.

Disneyland's parking lot in the 1960s!

★ A Lot of Changes

Out in Florida, there was oodles of available land but it wasn't the same story in California. Disneyland was so popular that many restaurants, shops and hotels had built up all around it. The Walt Disney Company wanted to turn Disneyland into a resort like the one in Florida but there was no room! But wait. Around Disneyland there were HUGE flat parking lots. What about there? Yes! It was the perfect solution. Tall, multi-level parking garages went up nearby and the old parking lots began to be turned into Disney's newest vacation destination. Downtown Disney's shops and restaurants, Disney's Grand Californian Hotel & Spa and Disney California Adventure all opened in 2001. California had its very own Disney resort at last!

FUN FACT

The Mickey & Friends Parking Structure can hold over 10,000 vehicles & when it opened in 2000, it was the largest parking structure in America.

WHEW!

2001
DCA opens with four lands: Golden State, Hollywood Pictures Backlot, Paradise Pier & Sunshine Plaza.

2007
Disney announces big plans for a billion-dollar makeover of Disney California Adventure.

2011
Welcome back! Disney California Adventure's Main Entrance gets a complete redesign.

2012
Disney California Adventure is rededicated & Guests enjoy all-new lands called Buena Vista Street & Cars Land.

★ Early Days

Disney California Adventure's official Opening Day was February 8th. Guests gathered in the **Esplanade** to enjoy a grand opening ceremony with dazzling special effects and live dance performances in front of large blue screens. After speeches from The Walt Disney Company executives Roy E. Disney and Michael Eisner, the screens moved to reveal the entrance to the brand new park! The park was divided into four lands and each one explored different California themes:

> SO YOU KNOW...
> Esplanade = large open area between the entrances to DCA and Disneyland

- Golden State

  Showcased the state's airfields, bays, farms and mountains
- Hollywood Pictures Backlot

  Highlighted the behind-the-scenes workings of the entertainment industry
- Paradise Pier

  Explored the West Coast's seaside carnival amusements
- Sunshine Plaza

  Celebrated California's pop and surf cultures

Even though DCA had only just opened, there were already plans in the works to add more attractions. A new land with rides for younger children called A Bug's Land opened in 2002, a new attraction called The Twilight Zone Tower of Terror opened in 2004 and another new attraction called Monsters, Inc. Mike & Sulley to the Rescue opened in 2006.

★ Top 6 Fun Spots Beyond the Parks

Check out these fun places in and around Downtown Disney!

#1 WORLD of DISNEY

This building with larger-than-life characters on the outside houses the largest Disney store on the entire West Coast! If you can't find a souvenir you like here, you're just not trying.

#2 anna & elsa's Boutique

Arendelle **aficionados** will love this wintry shop devoted to all things *Frozen*. Anna, Elsa and Olaf-themed makeovers for kids are the highlight.

> SO YOU KNOW...
> aficionados = fans

#3 Wonderground Gallery

This art gallery features unique Disney-inspired artwork and goods like magnet sets, plates, postcards and bags that you won't find in any other shop. The gallery often hosts artist appearances and other special events.

#4 Disney's Grand Californian Hotel

It's worth a look around this beautiful hotel even if you're not staying there. People-watch in the lobby as a live pianist tickles the ivories or pull up a mini rocking chair and enjoy classic cartoons.

#5 Goofy's Kitchen

Enjoy Mickey-shaped waffles with fun and lively Disney characters at Goofy's Kitchen in the Disneyland Hotel. PCH Grill in Paradise Pier Hotel and Storytellers Café in Disney's Grand Californian Hotel also offer Character Breakfasts.

#6 TRADER Sam's enchanted Tiki Bar

If you've taken a jungle cruise in Disneyland, you've surely encountered the headhunter Trader Sam who's willing to trade two of his heads for one of yours. This colorful watering hole is filled with exotic tropical treasures that move and change when people order certain drinks.

HOT TIP Located in the Disneyland Hotel, Trader Sam's is a **bar** but kids are allowed in **until 8 p.m.** as long as they sit at a **table** and not up at the bar.

★ Major Makeover

After DCA had been open for six years, Disney announced they would completely redo parts of the park and add a brand new land as part of a billion-dollar makeover. Instead of focusing on modern California culture, the park would explore special moments and places in the state's rich history—especially those that were tied to the legends and legacy of Walt Disney!

Photograph by Dave DeCaro • http://davelandweb.com

GOLDEN STATE POP QUIZ!

Disney California Adventure features loads of **California themes** but how well do **YOU** know this big, beautiful state? Put your knowledge to the test and put a ✔ in the box next to the correct answers below. Get **3–6** questions right and you're a **LOCAL**. Get **0–2** questions right and you're a **NEWBIE**. *Answers on page 182.*

1 What animal is featured on the California flag?
☐ Grizzly Bear   ☐ Panda Bear   ☐ Polar Bear

2 What is the state bird of California?
☐ California Flamingo   ☐ California Quail   ☐ California Seagull

3 What is the state capital of California?
☐ Los Angeles   ☐ Sacramento   ☐ San Diego

4 What is the state flower of California?
☐ California Pansy   ☐ California Poppy   ☐ California Sunflower

5 What is the state motto of California?
☐ Ay Carumba!   ☐ Eureka!   ☐ Surf's Up!

Walt Disney's California

THE WALT DISNEY STUDIOS
Current studio location since 1940
500 South Buena Vista Street

WALT DISNEY'S CAROLWOOD BARN
Actual barn from Walt's Carolwood home
5202 Zoo Drive

GRIFFITH PARK MERRY-GO-ROUND
One of Walt's inspirations for Disneyland
4730 Crystal Springs Drive

TAM O'SHANTER INN (RESTAURANT)
Ask to sit at table 31 —Walt's favorite!
2980 Los Feliz Boulevard

HOLLYWOOD WALK OF FAME
Walt has 2 stars— 1 for TV, 1 for film
6700 & 7000 block of Hollywood Boulevard

SITE OF THE WALT DISNEY STUDIOS
Location of studio from 1926–1940
2719 Hyperion Avenue

WALT DISNEY'S FIRST L.A. HOME
Walt moved in with his Uncle Robert
4406 Kingswell Avenue

LOS ANGELES THEATER
Inspiration for DCA's Hyperion Theater
615 South Broadway

HOLLY-VERMONT REALTY COMPANY
Walt & Roy rented office space in 1923
4451 Kingswell Avenue

SITE OF WALT'S LAST HOME
Featured his famous backyard railroad
355 Carolwood Drive

SITE OF CARTHAY CIRCLE THEATER
Location of premiere of *Snow White and the Seven Dwarfs*
6316 San Vicente Boulevard

SITE OF DISNEY BROS. STUDIO
Location of studio from 1924–1926
4647 Kingswell Avenue

UNCLE ROBERT'S GARAGE
Walt's first L.A. studio moved here for display
Stanley Ranch Museum

THE DISNEYLAND RESORT

BURBANK

GRIFFITH PARK

ATWATER VILLAGE

BEVERLY HILLS

HOLLYWOOD

SILVER LAKE

LOS FELIZ

WILSHIRE DISTRICT

DOWNTOWN LOS ANGELES

PACIFIC OCEAN

GARDEN GROVE

Los Angeles County

Orange County

If you stand here today and look towards DCA you'll see it's TOTALLY different!

★ Greetings from California

Originally, the entrance to DCA looked like a life-size postcard with 11.5-foot tall letters that spelled out CALIFORNIA, colorful mountains made of tile, a **replica** of the Golden Gate Bridge, and a Sun Icon sculpture that rose over a mesmerizing Wave Fountain. Through the entrance gates, a land called Sunshine Plaza was decorated with oversized postcards, neon lights and a parked train called the California Zephyr. As part of the big makeover, the entrance to the park was redesigned and Sunshine Plaza was transformed into beautiful Buena Vista Street.

HOT TIP These days, you can visit the **California Zephyr** train at its new home at the Western Pacific Railroad Museum in Portola, California. The **giant letters** are now on display at the Cal Expo in Sacramento, California.

PHony BaLoney!

All of these shops used to be in Sunshine Plaza—except for **one**. Can you put a ✔ in the box next to the fake? *Answer on page 182.*

☐ Baker's Field Bakery

☐ Candy Shoppe

☐ Engine-Ears Toys

☐ Bur-r-r Bank Ice Cream

☐ Daisy Duck's Depot

☐ Greetings from California

"And with that wonderful audacity of youth, I went to Hollywood, arriving there with just forty dollars. It was a big day the day I got on that Santa Fe California Limited. I was just free and happy!"
—WALT DISNEY

★ Inspired by Walt

Across the way in Disneyland, Walt Disney and the original Imagineers had created an inviting land called Main Street USA as the first area Guests would experience after entering. The Imagineers in charge of redesigning the entrance to Disney California Adventure wanted to create something just as special and they looked to Walt Disney for inspiration. In the 1920s, Walt arrived in Hollywood with little money and big dreams. Imagineers studied the unique buildings and landmarks from Walt's early days in Hollywood and used them as models for Buena Vista Street. The new land included an all-new attraction, Red Car Trolley and a statue of Walt with his best friend Mickey Mouse called Storytellers. From the all-new Main Entrance designed to look like the Pan-Pacific Auditorium to an impressive replica of the famous Carthay Circle Theatre, DCA now had an entrance as charming as the one in Disneyland. As you stroll down Buena Vista Street, it's easy to feel just like Walt Disney setting off for adventure in California, free and happy.

FUN FACT

The Pan-Pacific Auditorium was a Los Angeles hotspot for many years. The building was added to the National Register of Historic Places in 1978 & was seen in the movie "Xanadu" in 1980. Sadly, the building sat empty for years & was destroyed by an accidental fire in 1989.

TOO BAD!

EXAMPLES OF REAL-LIFE INSPIRATIONS

Found in Buena Vista Street	Found in Los Angeles
★ Atwater Ink & Paint	★ Atwater Village neighborhood
★ Disneyland Monorail bridge	★ Glendale-Hyperion Bridge
★ Kingswell Camera Shop	★ Kingswell Avenue
★ Los Feliz Five & Dime	★ Los Feliz Boulevard and neighborhood

SHoe SHOPPiNG!

Which character would buy which pair of "kicks" below: Alice, Anna, Cinderella, Honey Lemon, Jafar, Mickey Mouse, Tinker Bell or Woody? The first one's been done for you. *Answers on page 182.*

Alice

Answers on page 182.

"I'm in this little town called Radiator Springs. You know Route 66? It's still here!"
—LIGHTNING MCQUEEN

★ Get Your Kicks on Route 66

One of the most exciting all-new parts of the park was Cars Land, a new crown jewel for DCA. Route 66, which ran between California and Illinois, had its heyday in the 1950s and 60s. This famous American highway and its real-life retro diners, motels and gas stations were the inspiration behind the town of Radiator Springs first seen in the Disney•Pixar movie *Cars*. Cars Land recreated this town in amazing detail and opened with three new attractions—Luigi's Flying Tires, Mater's Junkyard Jamboree and Radiator Springs Racers, an instant fan favorite.

SPY See if you can spot the shape of **car tailfins** in Cars Land's mountains. At **Cadillac Ranch** in Texas, real Cadillac cars were half-buried **nose-first** in the ground as a **roadside attraction**.

---

eXaMPLeS of ReaL-Life iNSPiRaTioNS

Found in Cars Land	Found along Route 66
★ Cozy Cone Motel	★ Wigwam Motels in various states
★ Fillmore's Taste-In	★ Ortega's Indian Market in Arizona
★ Radiator Springs Curios	★ Hackberry General Store in Arizona
★ Ramone's House of Body Art	★ U-Drop Inn in Texas

RoaD TRiP!

Scattered below are the **8 states** that the historic Route 66 ran through. Fill in the **missing letters** from the names of each state. If you have your book with you in DCA, look on the wall of **Flo's V8 Café** for help with the answer. The first one's been done for you. *Answers on page 182.*

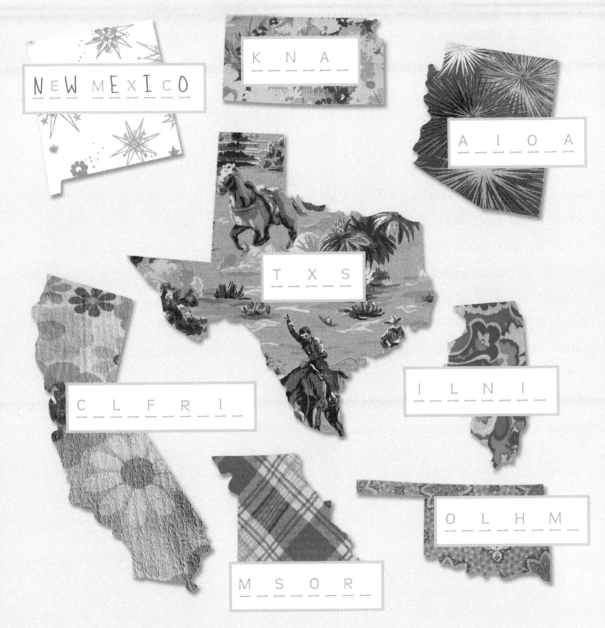

N E W   m E X I c O

K _ N _ A _

A _ I _ O _ A

T _ _ X _ _ S

I _ _ L _ N _ I

C _ L _ F _ R _ I _

M _ S _ O _ R _

O _ L _ H _ M _

BONUS QUESTION: *FOR GEOGRAPHY GENIUSES ONLY!*
List which order you would drive through these states if you started in **California** and headed east.

★ Another Day in Paradise

When DCA first opened, Paradise Pier looked like a wild and colorful beach boardwalk carnival. Guests plummeted towards the earth on a giant outdoor drop tower, spun inside an oversized orange and rotated around an enormous sun. When Imagineers began to redo this area they realized what was missing was Disney magic. The look of the entire land was changed to resemble a charming seaside amusement park—some attractions were removed and some attractions that stayed were given new themes that related more to Disney and less to California. Three brand new attractions were added—the super-fun Toy Story Midway Mania, the dazzling World of Color water-show spectacular and the enchanting Little Mermaid ~ Ariel's Undersea Adventure.

SPY

See if you can find **Ariel's sisters** on the outside of The Little Mermaid ~ Ariel's Undersea Adventure.

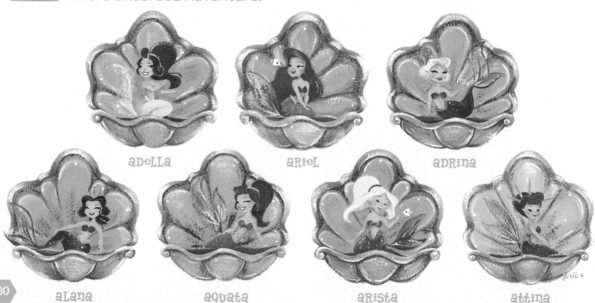

adella

ariel

adrina

alana

aquata

arista

attina

★ New Beginnings

In addition to the new entrance, Buena Vista Street, Cars Land and Paradise Pier changes, Hollywood Pictures Backlot was spruced up and given a new name—Hollywood Land. The large land known as Golden State was divided into Condor Flats, Grizzly Peak and Pacific Wharf. By 2012, DCA's big makeover was complete and the park was now divided into eight themed lands:

- A Bug's Land
- Buena Vista Street
- Cars Land
- Condor Flats ← *Rethemed in 2015 to become a part of Grizzly Peak!*
- Grizzly Peak
- Hollywood Land
- Pacific Wharf
- Paradise Pier

The night before the grand rededication ceremony on June 15th 2012, excited fans camped out in the Esplanade between Disneyland and Disney California Adventure. The ceremony took place in front of the new Carthay Circle Restaurant and included appearances by Red Car Trolley News Boys, Disney's CEO Robert Iger, Mickey Mouse and other Disney characters. Afterwards, Guests raced to check out the new Cars Land.

R.I.P.
SOME ATTRACTIONS THAT ARE GONERS

Bountiful Valley Farm
Water play area and farming exhibits—now the site of Mater's Junkyard Jamboree

Golden Dreams
Film about the history of California featuring Califia, Queen of California— now the site of The Little Mermaid ~ Ariel's Undersea Adventure

Maliboomer
Test Your Strength-themed freefall drop ride within the tracks of California Screamin'

Mission Tortilla Factory
Guests learned how tortillas are made and enjoyed samples —now the site of Ghirardelli's Soda Fountain and Chocolate Shop

Muppet*Vision 3D
3D film featured Kermit the Frog guiding Guests on a tour through Muppet Studios —now the site of Sunset Showcase Theater

Seasons of the Vine
Film about the history of winemaking in California —now the site of Walt Disney Imagineering Blue Sky Cellar

S.S. Rustworthy
Fireboat-themed Interactive water play area—now the site of the Boardwalk Pizza & Pasta seating area

Superstar Limo
Guests rode in stretch limos past comical displays of celebrities—now the site of Monsters, Inc. Mike & Sulley to the Rescue

Tisha as Flo

Sophie as Boo

DRESSING DISNEY

Visitors young and old love to get into the spirit and **dress up** when they visit Disney parks. Children can wear costumes anytime but people over **13 years old** aren't allowed to—except at certain Halloween events. Instead, many Guests enjoy **DisneyBounding**—a term that comes from Disney fan Leslie Kay's popular **DisneyBound blog** which shows how to dress like a Disney character using regular clothes. Many **DisneyBounders** create custom clothes or add special details to their outfits to enhance the theme. Lately, **clothing makers** have been getting in on the act too, offering clothes and accessories inspired by Disney characters. If **you** want to dress up like a Disney character, take a look in your closet and you **just might** have everything you need!

The Foster-Rileys as the gang from Inside Out

DisneyBound founder Leslie Kay

GUESS THE DISNEYBOUND!

Fill in the blanks with the **name of the character** you would look like if you wore these outfits: Ariel, Daisy Duck, Mickey Mouse, Robin Hood or Smee. The first one's been done for you. *Answers on page 182.*

1   +   +   =   Mickey Mouse

2   +   +   =

3   +   +   =

4   +   +   =

5   +   +   =

BONUS QUESTION:
Who is Leslie DisneyBounding as on the opposite page?_____

DCA is filled with special details like vintage automobile tail light flowers in Cars Land.

VISITING DCA

What Will You Find in This Chapter?

DISNEY CALIFORNIA ADVENTURE'S LANDS
See what the seven themed lands are all about

SO MUCH TO SEE & DO
Info on shows, live music and parades

JUST SOME OF THE SEASONAL FUN
Events that only happen at certain times of the year

ENTERTAINMENT AT A GLANCE
Handy chart of entertainment offerings

ATTRACTIONS AT A GLANCE
Handy chart of all attractions

HOW FASTPASS WORKS
The ins & outs of FastPass

FUN WITH CHARACTER
You'll find Disney characters all around DCA

CHARACTER HANGOUTS
Where to look for characters

CHARACTER COLOR SCHEMES!
Which colors go with which character?

FOOD & DRINKS AT A GLANCE
Handy chart with info on food & drinks

TOP 6 SCRUMPTIOUS SNACKS
The best snacks & treats

SHOPS AT A GLANCE
Handy chart of all shops

STACK ATTACK
The stacking fun of Tsum Tsums

SAY "CHEESE!"
Info on PhotoPass

TOP 7 SHOPS
Shops worth going in whether you're shopping or not

TOP 5 TIPS FOR VISITING WITH LITTLES
Things to know if you or someone you know is a baby or small child

SAY WHAT? KID EDITION!
Which character said what

WHERE'S MICKEY?
A brief rundown on Hidden Mickeys

TOP 4 PLACES TO BEAT THE HEAT
Where to cool off on a hot day

WHERE TO FIND FROSTY TREATS
Cool snacks and where to find them

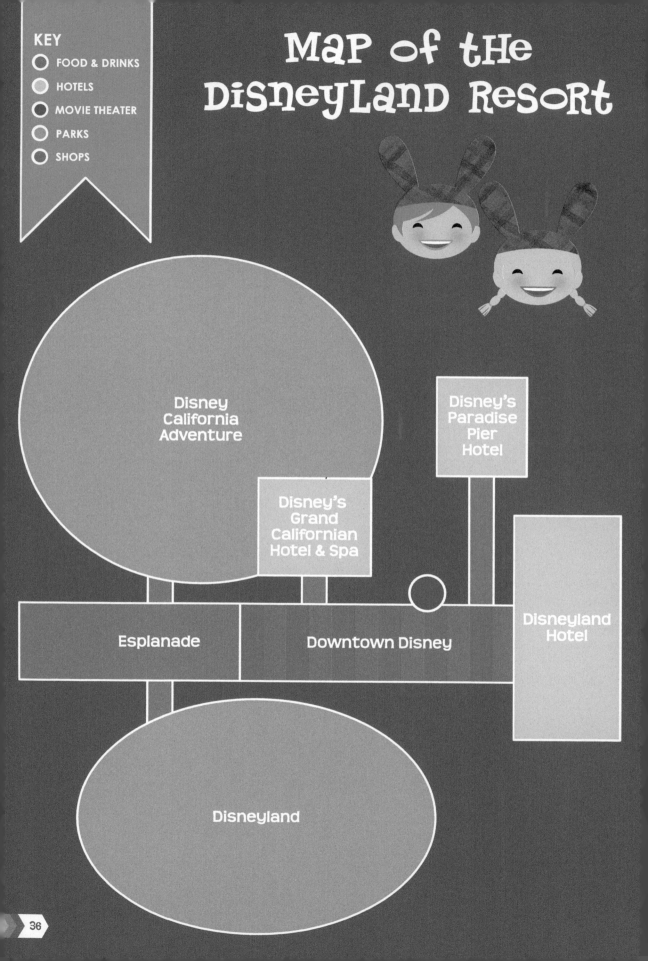

MaP of tHE DISNEYLAND ResoRt

KEY
- FOOD & DRINKS
- HOTELS
- MOVIE THEATER
- PARKS
- SHOPS

Disney California Adventure

Disney's Paradise Pier Hotel

Disney's Grand Californian Hotel & Spa

Esplanade

Downtown Disney

Disneyland Hotel

Disneyland

California Adventures

So, you're off to DCA?! Dandy! The park sits on 72 acres in the Disneyland Resort and is open every single day of the year—even Thanksgiving and Christmas. Though Disney sells one-day tickets, many visitors spend multiple days at the Resort. Some people like to go to Disneyland one day and Disney California Adventure the next. Other Guests like to go back and forth using Park Hopper tickets. For mega-Disney fans, there are also five-day tickets and different types of Annual Passports—some that are good for every day of the year. However long you stay, you're sure to have a grand time!

★ 7 Themed Lands

Disney California Adventure's lands each have their own theme and unique look. If you've already been to DCA, put a ✓ by your fave! If you've never ever been to DCA, put a ✓ by the land you think you'll like best when you get there.

☐ A Bug's Land
☐ Buena Vista Street
☐ Cars Land
☐ Grizzly Peak
☐ Hollywood Land
☐ Pacific Wharf
☐ Paradise Pier

DISNEY CALIFORNIA ADVENTURE'S LANDS

PACIFIC WHARF
Inspired by waterfront fishing areas in Northern California, this land full of restaurants is the place to visit when you're looking for a bite!

PARADISE PIER
Delight in old-fashioned seaside amusements. Catch a ride on a coastal coaster, hop on a smiling sea creature and take aim in carnival games!

RAIL ROAD CROSSING

BUENA VISTA STREET
Travel back in time to the Golden Age of Hollywood. Enjoy beautiful buildings, quaint shops and a cheery cherry-colored trolley to whisk you away to your next adventure!

GRIZZLY PEAK

Rush down a roaring river, soar over scenic sights and wander through a woodsy wonderland in this national park-themed land!

ROUTE
66

CARS LAND

Motor through Radiator Springs to spin, zip and zoom on cars and tractors!

A BUG'S LAND

Live "a bug's life" in this leafy land where you can spin in a ladybug, chomp with a caterpillar and fly with an inventive ant!

HOLLYWOOD LAND

Stroll the boulevards and rub elbows with furry monsters, sweet princesses and super-nice super heroes!

> "I would rather entertain and hope that people learned something than educate people and hope they were entertained."
> –WALT DISNEY

★ So Much to See & Do

Disney California Adventure has attractions, shops and restaurants. But that's **not** all! There are also live shows, bands, singers, dancers, parades, seasonal events, characters to meet and special tours to take. When you walk in the Main Entrance, you can get a Map of the park and an Entertainment Times Guide with info on stage shows, live entertainment and character Meet n' Greets.

 HOT TIP The **Disneyland Resort app** is a free, fabulous way to get **up-to-the-minute info** on shows, wait times and character locations.

 SPY Free **Buena Vista Bugle** newspapers with park info can be found in the **Chamber of Commerce** and various spots around Buena Vista Street.

HEY KIDS COLOR ME IN!

The Buena Vista Bugle — VISITING DCA — A GREAT IDEA!

Photograph by Dave DeCaro • http://davelandweb.com

Just Some of the Seasonal Fun

WINTER
- Buena Vista Street Holiday Tree Lighting
- World of Color winter-themed show
- Disney !Viva Navidad! includes Mexican-themed dancing, music and more
- Meet Santa Claus
- Three Kings Day (Dia de los Reyes Magos) includes crafts, traditional treats and displays
- Happy Lunar New Year Celebration includes live performers, musicians and local artisans

SPRING
- Valentine's Day decorations, treats and menus
- Easter egg scavenger hunt

SUMMER
- 4th of July festivities include military band performances and a pyrotechnic water display at the start of World of Color

FALL
- Halloween trick-or-treat stations, decorations, treats and menus

entertainment at a GLance

BUENA VISTA STREET

- Citizens of Buena Vista Street
- Five & Dime

HOLLYWOOD LAND

- Disney Junior Dance Party
- Frozen — Live at the Hyperion

A BUG'S LAND

- It's Tough to be a Bug

CARS LAND

- DJ's Dance 'n' Drive

PACIFIC WHARF

- Mariachi Divas

PARADISE PIER

- Operation: Playtime
- Paradise Garden Bandstand
- World of Color

MULTIPLE LANDS

- Pixar Play Parade
- Red Car Trolley News Boys

➡ Entertainment offerings and times often change so be sure to check current info.

➡ DCA's Entertainment Times Guide handout does not include info on everything that may be going on. If you have questions, head to the Chamber of Commerce or ask a friendly Cast Member.

➡ There's no regularly scheduled entertainment in Grizzly Peak at this time.

attractions at a glance

Map doesn't include ALL paths!

PARADISE PIER

CARS LAND

PACIFIC WHARF

PARADISE BAY

A BUG'S LAND

HOLLYWOOD LAND

BUENA VISTA STREET

GRIZZLY PEAK

ENTRANCE

BUENA VISTA STREET
• Red Car Trolley

A BUG'S LAND
• Flik's Flyers
• Francis' Ladybug Boogie
• Heimlich's Chew Chew Train
• Tuck and Roll's Drive 'Em Buggies

PARADISE PIER
• California Screamin'
• Golden Zephyr
• Goofy's Sky School
• Jumpin' Jellyfish
• King Triton's Carousel
• Mickey's Fun Wheel
• Silly Symphony Swings
• The Little Mermaid ~ Ariel's Undersea Adventure
• Toy Story Midway Mania

HOLLYWOOD LAND
• Disney Animation Building
• Guardians of the Galaxy — Mission: BREAKOUT
• Monsters, Inc. Mike & Sulley to the Rescue
• Red Car Trolley

CARS LAND
• Luigi's Rollickin' Roadsters
• Mater's Junkyard Jamboree
• Radiator Springs Racers

GRIZZLY PEAK
• Grizzly River Run
• Redwood Creek Challenge Trail
• Soarin' Around the World

HEIGHT REQUIREMENTS

For safety reasons, you have to be a certain height or taller to ride some attractions.

- 32" or taller   Luigi's Rollickin' Roadsters
  Mater's Junkyard Jamboree
- 36" or taller   Tuck and Roll's Drive 'Em Buggies
- 40" or taller   Guardians of the Galaxy — Mission:
  BREAKOUT
  Jumpin' Jellyfish
  Radiator Springs Racers
  Soarin' Around the World
- 40"-48"   Silly Symphony Swings (double swing)
- 42"-63"   Sequoia Smokejumpers Training Tower
  in Redwood Creek Challenge Trail
- 42" or taller   Cliff Hanger Traverse Rock Climb
  in Redwood Creek Challenge Trail
  Goofy's Sky School
  Grizzly River Run
- 48" or taller   California Screamin'
  Silly Symphony Swings (single swing)

SINGLE RIDER LINES

When Cast Members need someone to fill an empty spot on a ride, they pull people from the Single Rider line. This line usually moves faster than the regular line but you may be separated from others in your group.

- California Screamin'
- Goofy's Sky School
- Grizzly River Run
- Radiator Springs Racers

CLOSED DURING WORLD OF COLOR SHOWTIMES

- California Screamin' • Games of the Boardwalk
- Golden Zephyr • King Triton's Carousel
- Jumpin' Jellyfish • Mickey's Fun Wheel
- Silly Symphony Swings

RIDER SWITCH

One Guest waits with a non-rider while the rest of the group enjoys the ride. Then the Guest that waited uses a pass to ride alone or with one other person without having to go back in line.

- California Screamin'
- Goofy's Sky school
- Grizzly River Run
- Guardians of the Galaxy
  Mission: BREAKOUT
- Jumpin' Jellyfish
- Luigi's Rollickin' Roadsters
- Mater's Junkyard Jamboree
- Radiator Springs Racers
- Silly Symphony Swings
- Soarin' Around the World
- Tuck and Roll's Drive 'Em Buggies

FASTPASS

See "How FastPass Works" below.

- California Screamin'
- Frozen — Live at the Hyperion
- Goofy's Sky school
- Grizzly River Run
- Guardians of the Galaxy —
  Mission: BREAKOUT
- Radiator Springs Racers
- Soarin' Around the World
- Toy Story Midway Mania
- World of Color

NOTE: Some rides with height requirements have future FastPasses for kids. Once children are tall enough, they bring the pass back to enjoy the ride with their group.

HoW FastPass WorKs

#1   Find the **FastPass machines** that go with the attraction you want to experience.

#2   Check the **return time range** and, if it looks good, stick your **admission ticket** into a FastPass machine. Keep in mind, everyone in your group needs to have their **own** FastPass.

#3   The machine will give you a free **FastPass** with your return time printed on it. Be sure to get your admission ticket back too.

#4   When your return time arrives, go in the attraction's **FastPass line**.

Choose wisely. Attractions run out of FastPasses as the day goes on and, when you get a FastPass, you can't always get another one right away. Take a look at the **bottom** of your FastPass to see what time you can get another one.

Fun With Character

Disney California Adventure is filled with beloved Disney characters. You might happen upon a *lucky* long-eared fellow from one of the first cartoons Walt Disney ever created or spot a dapper *duck* dressed in his super-cute sailor suit. Some characters are in fixed *Meet n' Greet* locations while others roam around the park. If you meet a character, you can get your *photo* taken together and ask them for their autograph (*see page 172*). Some characters will sign their name with a pen and others have a *special stamp*. Characters can be seen in attractions, shows and parades, and character *themes* are found on souvenirs, menu items and more.

CHARACTER HANGOUTS

Here's where to look for characters in DCA. Fixed Meet n' Greet locations are marked with a ✱.

BUENA VISTA STREET

Near Main Entrance
• Oswald the Lucky Rabbit

Near Carthay Circle
• Chip 'n Dale • Daisy • Donald
• Goofy • Mickey • Minnie • Pluto

HOLLYWOOD LAND

Near Disney Junior Dance Party
• Doc McStuffins • Jake
• Sofia the First

Near Sunset Showcase Theater
• Judy Hopps • Nick Wilde • Olaf

Near Monsters, Inc. Mike & Sulley to the Rescue:
• Mike • Sulley

Across from Studio Catering Co. ✱
• Captain America • Spider-Man

In Disney Animation Building ✱
• Anna • Elsa

A BUG'S LAND

Near Princess Dot Puddle Park
• Flik

CARS LAND

Near Cozy Cone Motel ✱
• Lightning McQueen • Mater

Near Luigi's Rollickin' Roadsters
• Red the Fire Engine

PARADISE PIER

In Ariel's Grotto (Character Dining) ✱
• Ariel & other princesses

Across from Mickey's Fun Wheel ✱
• Buzz Lightyear • Jessie • Woody

GRIZZLY PEAK

In Redwood Creek Challenge Trail
• Carl Fredricksen • Dug • Russell

Near Grizzly River Run
• Chip 'n Dale

Near Soarin' Around the World
• Minnie • Pluto

CHARACTER COLOR SCHEMES!

Which **colors** go with which **character**: Anna, Ariel, Belle, Chip, Daisy Duck, Donald Duck, Goofy, Judy Hopps, Mickey Mouse, Minnie Mouse, Nemo, Peter Pan, Pluto, Sulley, Russell or Woody. The first one's been done for you.

Answers on page 182.

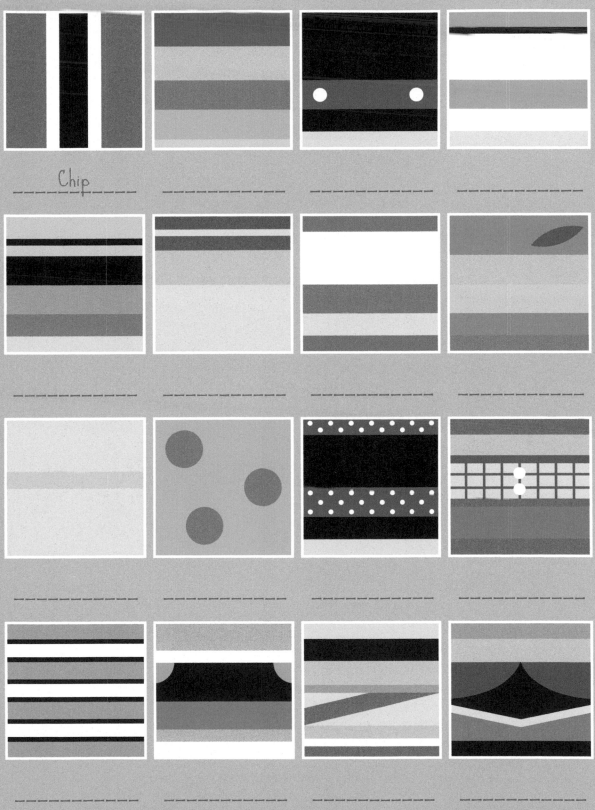

Chip

FOOD & DRINKS at a GLANCE

◆ = Open for breakfast

FULL SERVICE *Sit-down meal with waiters*	QUICK SERVICE *Order then take food to a table*	ON THE GO *Limited or no seating*

BUENA VISTA STREET

• Carthay Circle Lounge • Carthay Circle Restaurant	• Fiddler, Fifer & Practical Café ◆ 	• Clarabelle's Hand-Scooped Ice Cream • Mortimer's Market

HOLLYWOOD LAND

		• Award Wieners • Fairfax Market • Schmoozies • Studio Catering Co.

CARS LAND

	• Cozy Cone Motel ◆ • Flo's V8 Café ◆	• Fillmore's Taste-In

PACIFIC WHARF

• Alfresco Tasting Terrace • Mendocino Terrace • Wine Country Trattoria	• Cocina Cucamonga Mexican Grill • Ghirardelli Soda Fountain and Chocolate Shop • Lucky Fortune Cookery • Pacific Wharf Café • Sonoma Terrace	• Pacific Wharf Distribution Co. • Rita's Baja Blenders

PARADISE PIER

• Ariel's Grotto ◆ • Cove Bar 	• Boardwalk Pizza & Pasta • Corn Dog Castle • Paradise Garden Grill	• Bayside Brews • Don Tomas • Hot Dog Hut • Paradise Pier Ice Cream Co.

GRIZZLY PEAK

	• Smokejumpers Grill 	

⇨ There are also lots of snack carts and food stands

⇨ A Bug's Land has a few snack carts but no other food & drinks

⇨ The Baby Care Center (near Ghirardelli Soda Fountain and Chocolate Shop) has a filtered water refill station

⇨ Most quick-service and on-the-go places will give you free tap water in a to-go cup

⇨ Many restaurants have crowd-pleasing kids' menus

⇨ Mickey Check meals are prepared with lower calories and less saturated fat, sodium and sugar, and are marked with a special checkmark symbol on menus

Top 6 Scrumptious Snacks

Just like the state of California, Disney California Adventure is famous for its fabulous food. Which yummy taste treat sounds good to you?

#1 PRETZEL BITES

Dip itty-bitty bits of soft pretzel topped with salt into gooey cheese sauce—yesssssss!
LOCATION: Cozy Cone Motel

#2 FLAVORED POPCORN

Pop in to see what flavors are being served up. Which one do you hope for— Buffalo Ranch, Butter, Dill Pickle, Garlic Parmesan, Pizza, Sriracha or White Cheddar?
LOCATION: Cozy Cone Motel

#3 CHILI CONE QUESO

If you've never eaten something out of cone-shaped bread, you haven't lived! Beef OR vegetarian chili is topped with cheddar cheese and corn chips for a snack so hearty it can pass for a meal.
LOCATION: Cozy Cone Motel

#4 SWEET SUNDAE

Pop Quiz! What do you call it when you top bananas with scoops of vanilla, strawberry and chocolate ice cream, and add crushed pineapple, sliced strawberries, handmade hot fudge, chopped almonds, whipped cream and a cherry on top? The Golden Gate Banana Split!
LOCATION: Ghirardelli Soda Fountain and Chocolate Shop

#5 LOBSTER NACHOS

If you love lobster and nachos and looking out over amazing views of Paradise Bay, this is the snack for you!
LOCATION: Cove Bar

#6 SOFT-SERVE

Ice cream is great but there's just something SO great about soft-serve ice cream. Soft-serve is lighter and softer than regular ice cream because air is added to the mix while it's being frozen. Choose chocolate or vanilla —or both twisted together—and whether you want your ice cream dipped in chocolate.
LOCATION: Paradise Pier Ice Cream Co.

 HOT TIP **Cozy Cone Motel** also has soft serve but you can only get **chocolate-dipped** cones at **Paradise Pier Ice Cream Co.**

SHOPS at a Glance

BUENA VISTA STREET

- Atwater Ink & Paint
- Big Top Toys
- Elias & Co.
- Julius Katz & Sons
- Kingswell Camera Shop
- Los Feliz Five & Dime
- Oswald's
- Trolley Treats

HOLLYWOOD LAND

- Gone Hollywood
- Guardians of the Galaxy Gift Shop
- Off the Page
- Studio Store

CARS LAND

- Lube-O-Rama
- Radiator Springs Curios
- Ramone's House of Body Art
- Sarge's Surplus Hut

PARADISE PIER

- Boardwalk Bazaar
- Embarcadero Gifts
- Midway Mercantile
- Point Mugu Tattoo
- Seaside Souvenirs
- Sideshow Shirts
- Treasures in Paradise

GRIZZLY PEAK

- Humphrey's Service & Supplies
- Rushin' River Outfitters

⇨ There are also various carts and stands that sell souvenirs

⇨ A Bug's Land has no shops

⇨ Pacific Wharf has no shops but Ghirardelli Soda Fountain and Chocolate Shop does sell some souvenirs and gifts

Photographs by Dave DeCaro • http://davelandweb.com

Stack Attack

If there's one thing we can all agree on, it's that Tsum Tsum toys are adorable. The name comes from the Japanese word "tsumu" which means "to stack." The Tsum Tsum craze started out as a video game where players connect stacked Disney characters together. Tsum Tsum toys were first sold in Japan in 2013 and came to the U.S. a year later where they have become wildly popular. The toys come in different sizes and in a variety of characters from movies, short cartoons and even theme park attractions. Tsum Tsum fans collect these toys and display them stacked on top of each other in towers and pyramids. The mega-cute look of these toys has become so popular that you can find Tsum Tsum themes on pins, clothes, housewares and more!

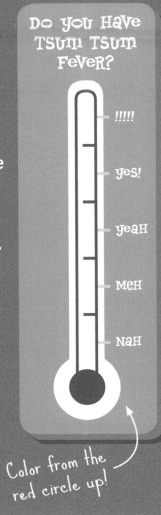

Do You Have Tsum Tsum Fever?

!!!!!

Yes!

Yeah

Meh

Nah

Color from the red circle up!

Say "Cheese!"

Friendly **Disney PhotoPass photographers** in tan vests are stationed throughout Disney California Adventure. For a fee, you can buy prints of the pictures they take of you in photo spots and on select rides from **Kingswell Camera Shop** or from the **Disneyland Resort website**. If you're interested, the first photographer you meet will give you a **PhotoPass card** with your account number. Each time you have your picture taken, give your card to the photographer. You can also ask the photographers to set up a **Magic Shot** pose where characters are added to the image **after** it's been taken. They are also happy to take photos of you with your **own** camera.

★ Top 7 Shops

Have fun looking for the perfect souvenir—or just looking!

#1 BIG TOP TOYS

Dumbo the Elephant performed in the **Big Top**—the name for the main tent in a circus. You'll feel like you're at the circus when you visit this cozy treasure trove of toys tucked under the Disneyland Monorail bridge in **Buena Vista Street.**

#2 eLiaS & Co.

This glamorous Art Deco-style department store in **Buena Vista Street** is Disney California Adventure's largest shop and carries a wide variety of goods for men, women and children. From the outside, Elias & Co. looks like many separate stores but inside they're all connected. Elias was Walt Disney's father's name AND Walt's middle name.

#3 Off tHe PaGe

Can you say Churrigueresque? Chur-rig-uer-esque! That's the name for the fancy Spanish Baroque-style architecture you'll see at this spot that specializes in high-end Disney collectibles in **Hollywood Land.** The interior of this shop is like an animator's studio come to life and is filled with unique artwork, statues and limited-edition souvenirs.

SPY Look on the ground in front of the **main door** to Off the Page to see a sketch of **Dumbo!**

#4 RADIATOR SPRINGS CURIOS

Pull off the main drag in **Cars Land** to visit Lizzie's rustic roadside shop that's decorated with weathered road signs, glowing neon lights and vintage gas pumps. **Curios** are unusual objects and this store carries some *Cars*-themed goods you probably won't see in other shops.

 HOT TIP The **old-fashioned red cooler** on the front porch of Radiator Springs Curios isn't just for looks. Open it up and reach in if you're in the market for an **icy-cold soda**.

#5 EMBARCADERO GIFTS

Are you really a mermaid? Then you'll definitely want to swim into this little aqua-and-pink jewelbox of a shop in **Paradise Pier** to comb through undersea treasures Ariel herself would adore. The name for this shop comes from a famous waterfront area in San Francisco called The Embarcadero.

EMBARCADERO GIFTS

#6 RUSHIN' RIVER OUTFITTERS

California's Russian River was the inspiration behind the name for this rustic **Grizzly Peak** shop outfitted with rugged canoes, mountain bikes and snow gear. Go wild exploring a large selection of nature-themed goods and supplies.

#7 HUMPHREY'S SERVICE & SUPPLIES

This **Grizzly Peak** shop is named after Humphrey the Bear who starred in short cartoons in the 1950s. Here you'll find a variety of automobile, aviation, national park and nature-themed goods. The shop looks like a quaint general store you'd find on a drive through California's mountain towns.

 HOT TIP Tucked right next to Humphrey's Service & Supplies is a **refreshment stand** with a huge variety of flavored sodas.

★ Top 5 Tips for Visiting with Littles

Helpful hints for heading to DCA with babies and small children from Instagram superstars—and sisters—Julie and Emily of Magic Kingdom Mamas.

#1 Visit the Baby Care Center

This helpful spot in Pacific Wharf has changing tables, highchairs, kid-sized potties and areas for nursing babies. You can also buy essential items you may have forgotten like baby food, diapers, formula, pacifiers, sunscreen, wipes and even some over-the-counter meds.

#2 Let them Run Free

A day in DCA brings with it plenty of fun but also lots of waiting in lines and stroller time for little ones. The best places to let kids have some playtime:

- Animation Courtyard
- Princess Dot Puddle Park
- Redwood Creek Challenge Trail

#3 Have an Emergency Plan

For safety and ease of mind, make sure your contact info is somewhere on your kids in case they are separated from you. This is a good idea even if your child has memorized your phone number as they may forget it if they are lost and scared. There are a number of ways to do this:

- Pick up a free emergency contact sticker at the Baby Care Center
- Record the info on a piece of paper and put it into their shoe or pocket
- Use an Emergency Contact Temporary Tattoo from Madeline's Box (available online)
- Write info on your child's arm and cover it with a liquid bandage

#4 Ask about Options

If your child has dietary restrictions, DCA has got you covered! Most eateries offer allergy-free menus and any food-service facility will do its best to accommodate dietary restrictions when requests are made, even sending the chef out to speak to Guests if necessary.

#5 Bring Fun

Bring a few items to keep your kids entertained while waiting in line like bubbles, favorite toys, teething necklaces, snacks and—if necessary—lollipops!

Photograph by Jacqui Saldana

say WHat? KiD eDition!

Guess **which** Disney little one said **what**.
Draw a **speech bubble** from their name to the quote.
The first one's been done for you. *Answers on page 182.*

The sky's awake so I'm awake!

He flewed!

I'll do anything to stay in the jungle!

Anna

Baby Dory

Can I try?
I have a robot
I built it myself.

Hiro Hamada

Michael Darling

Are you going to eat me?

Mowgli

But father,
I'm alive. See?

Pete

Pinocchio

I suffer
from short-term
remembery
loss.

Riley

I know you
don't want me to,
but I miss home.

WHeRe'S MiCKeY?

There are **loads** of **Hidden Mickeys** in DCA. Put a ✓ in the box next to the ones you see. Not sure what a Hidden Mickey is? Turn to the **Disney Dictionary** on page 8.

BUENA VISTA STREET:

☐ On the floor outside the entrance to Carthay Circle Restaurant
NOTE: Look to the right of the main door.

You never know where you might spy a Hidden Mickey!

☐ On the cows on the milk bottles at Clarabelle's Hand-Scooped Ice Cream

HOLLYWOOD LAND:

☐ One of Sulley's purple spots in Monsters, Inc. Mike & Sulley to the Rescue

☐ On the top of the flagpole on Disney Animation Building

A BUG'S LAND:

☐ On a wall near the end of Heimlich's Chew Chew Train

CARS LAND:

☐ On a wall in line for Mater's Junkyard Jamboree

☐ On a car hood inside Ramone's House of Body Art

PARADISE PIER:

☐ On top of a wrench hanging on a rack near the Goofy's Sky School exit

☐ On the support poles for Jumpin' Jellyfish

GRIZZLY PEAK:

☐ On the map for Redwood Creek Challenge Trail

Want to search for even more Mickeys? The website **www.FindingMickey.com** lists lots more to find. HAPPY HUNTING...

Top 4 Places to Beat the Heat

Feeling the heat? Cool down in these refreshing areas!

#1 animation COurtyard

Sure, all indoor attractions have air conditioning but, unlike a ride, you can hang out in this lobby as long as you like, enjoying Disney clips on several huge screens until you're ready to brave the heat again.

LOCATION: Hollywood Land

#2 PRincess Dot PUDDLe PARK

Play in the water under a giant, leaky garden hose in this shady, green escape.

LOCATION: A Bug's Land

#3 SPLASH PaD at PARADise PARK

This splash pad's fountains aren't always running but, when they are, it's a great place to cool off.

LOCATION: Paradise Pier

#4 GRIZZLy RiVeR Run

There's a good chance you'll get wet on this rousing ride. Even if you're not rolling down the river, head to the bridge that spans over the water to enjoy the cool mist and splashes as the rafts blast by.

LOCATION: Grizzly Peak

WHeRe to FinD FRosty TReats

HOLLYWOOD LAND:
Smoothie from Schmoozies

A BUG'S LAND:
Frozen Fruity Drink from
 Fun and Fruity Drink Cart

CARS LAND:
Milkshake from Flo's V8 Café

Red's Apple Freeze, "Route" Beer Float
 or Ice Cream from Cozy Cone Motel

PACIFIC WHARF:
Tropicool Frozen Drink
 from Rita's Baja Blenders

PARADISE PIER:
Ice Cream from Paradise
 Pier Ice Cream Co.

GRIZZLY PEAK:
Milkshake from
 Smokejumpers Grill

THROUGHOUT THE PARK AT VARIOUS SNACK CARTS:
Frozen drinks, frozen fruit, ice cream & popsicles

Grab a booth and enjoy the vintage charm of Fiddler, Fifer & Practical Café.

Buena Vista Street

What Will You Find in This Chapter?

ATTRACTIONS
- Red Car Trolley

ENTERTAINMENT
- Citizens of Buena Vista Street
- Five & Dime
- Red Car Trolley News Boys

FOOD & DRINKS
- Carthay Circle Lounge
- Carthay Circle Restaurant
- Clarabelle's Hand-Scooped Ice Cream
- Fiddler, Fifer & Practical Café
- Mortimer's Market

SHOPS
- Atwater Ink & Paint
- Big Top Toys
- Elias & Co.
- Julius Katz & Sons
- Kingswell Camera Shop
- Los Feliz Five & Dime
- Oswald's
- Trolley Treats

ACTIVITIES, GAMES & INFO
- Bustling Buena Vista Street
- The Lucky Rabbit
- Buena Vista Street Scavenger Hunt!
- Gone But Not Forgotten
- Story Time
- Sample Souvenirs
- Nine Old Men & One Special Young Lady
- Who Shops Where?

Map of Buena Vista Street

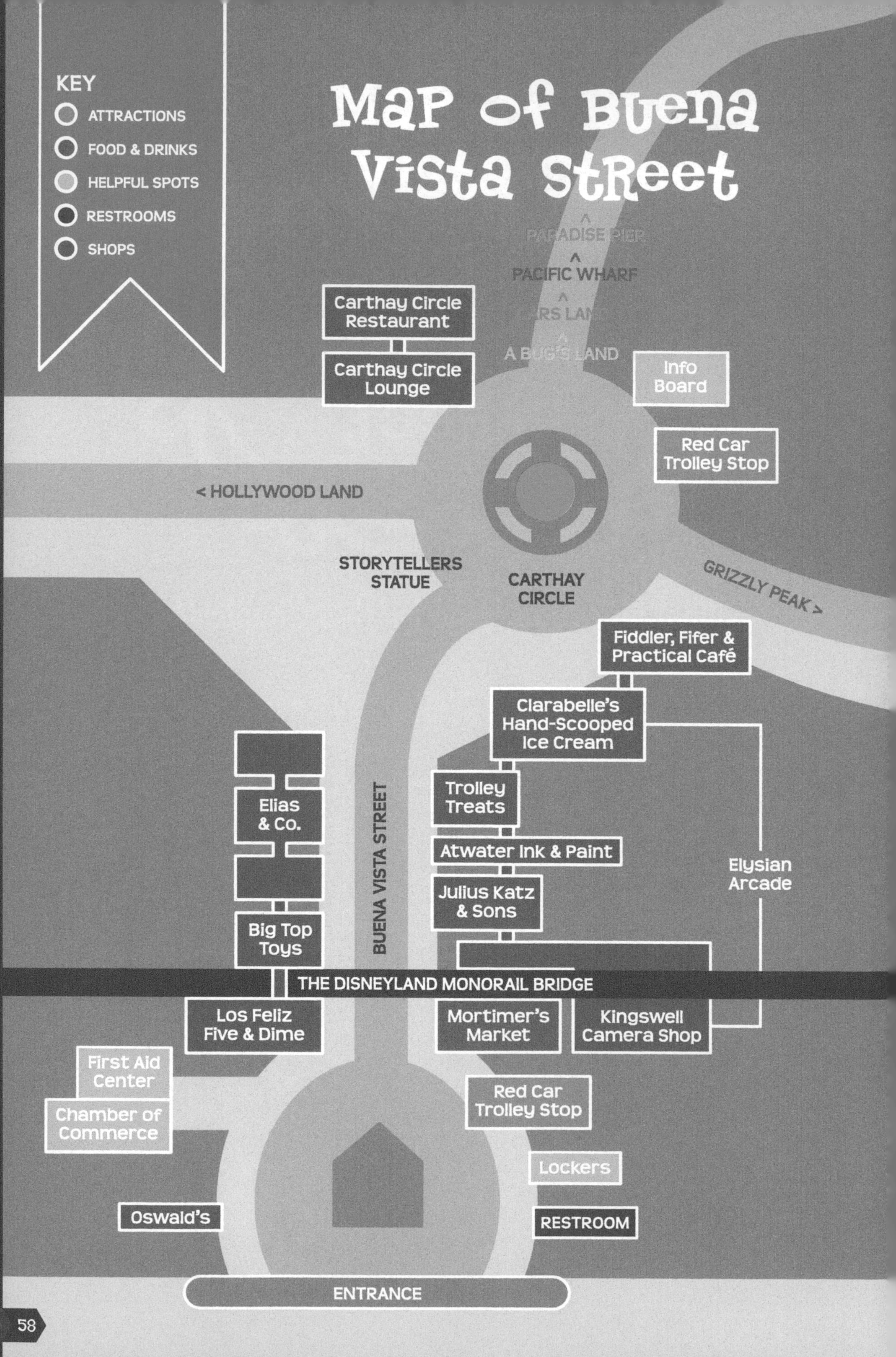

KEY
- ○ ATTRACTIONS
- ○ FOOD & DRINKS
- ○ HELPFUL SPOTS
- ○ RESTROOMS
- ○ SHOPS

^ PARADISE PIER

^ PACIFIC WHARF

^ CARS LAND

^ A BUG'S LAND

Carthay Circle Restaurant

Carthay Circle Lounge

Info Board

Red Car Trolley Stop

< HOLLYWOOD LAND

STORYTELLERS STATUE

CARTHAY CIRCLE

GRIZZLY PEAK >

Fiddler, Fifer & Practical Café

Clarabelle's Hand-Scooped Ice Cream

Elias & Co.

Trolley Treats

Atwater Ink & Paint

Julius Katz & Sons

Elysian Arcade

BUENA VISTA STREET

Big Top Toys

THE DISNEYLAND MONORAIL BRIDGE

Los Feliz Five & Dime

Mortimer's Market

Kingswell Camera Shop

First Aid Center

Chamber of Commerce

Red Car Trolley Stop

Lockers

Oswald's

RESTROOM

ENTRANCE

A Good View

It's easy to imagine yourself in the Los Angeles of yesteryear as you meander past the retro gas station, elegant shops and charming eateries of beautiful Buena Vista Street. This land harkens back to the Los Angeles of the 1920s and 30s. The name—which means "good view" in Spanish—comes from Buena Vista Street in Burbank in Northern Los Angeles where the Walt Disney Studios have been located since 1940. To travel through this lovely land, stroll towards the fountain in Carthay Circle or hop on a trolley headed for nearby Hollywood Land.

CHAIR!

Banana!

ARROW!

Waiting Game!

ALPHA HUNT
Working together, look for something that starts with the letter "A" then "B" then "C" and so on until you reach the end of the alphabet. Take your time and find things throughout the day as you move from place to place. You may have to get creative when you get to letters like "Q" and "Z"!

★ Bustling Buena Vista Street

CHAMBER of COMMERCE

Just inside the entrance gates is the oh-so-helpful **Chamber of Commerce**. Like Disneyland's City Hall, this Guest Relations center can assist you with character locations, reservations, show times, tours and info about anything and everything you may want to know. If you're celebrating a birthday, first visit or other occasion, pop in for a free button.

 The Chamber of Commerce often has fun handouts like **Pressed Coin Location Guides.**

SO YOU KNOW...
Chamber of Commerce = local organization that supports businesses in a community

FIRST AID CENTER

Located right next door to the Chamber of Commerce, friendly nurses are standing by in case you need basic medical assistance, medicine or Mickey Mouse bandages.

LOCKERS

For a fee, you can rent a locker for the day—and some even have charging stations to recharge various devices.

 There are **also** lockers in between the two parks and in Disneyland.

THE LUCKY RABBIT

Have you ever heard of **Oswald the Lucky Rabbit?** He can often be found in DCA near the Main Entrance but many Guests see Oswald and wonder **"Who is that?!"** In 1927 the Walt Disney Studios created short cartoons starring a long-eared rabbit named Oswald—this was even before **Mickey Mouse** had come onto the scene. In recent times, Oswald was featured in the video game series *Epic Mickey* and had a **small part** in the short Mickey Mouse cartoon *Get a Horse!* Though you'll sometimes see Oswald's wife **Ortensia the Cat** featured on souvenirs in the park, she herself has not stopped by DCA—yet.

Buena Vista Street Scavenger Hunt!

When the Imagineers created Buena Vista Street, they included many special details to honor Disney history. To go along with the Spanish name of this land, say **"Ahi esta!"** ("There it is!") when you spot these sights. Put a ✓ in the box next to the ones you find.

Each name on this mailbox has meaning—like E. Valiant for Eddie Valiant, a character in *Who Framed Roger Rabbit*

Gunther Lessing, Kay Kamen and Cyril James were lawyers and businessmen who worked for Disney

Holly-Vermont Realty rented young Walt & his brother Roy space in their office on Kingswell Avenue

Rock Candy Mountain was planned but never actually made as part of Disneyland's Storybook Land attraction

Rows and rows of colorful jars of paint just like a Disney Ink and Paint artist might have used to color in animation cels

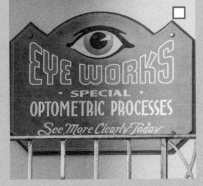

Ub Iwerks (pronounced "eye works") was an animator who helped Walt create Oswald and Mickey Mouse cartoons

BONUS ROUND:

FUN FACT

Red Car Trolleys were featured in the movie "Who Framed Roger Rabbit" which was set in Los Angeles in 1947.

DING! DING!

SUNSET BOULEVARD

CARTHAY CIRCLE

HOLLYWOOD BOULEVARD

MAIN ENTRANCE

★ Red Car Trolley

STREETCAR VEHICLES · EST. 2012 · CALM & MELLOW

When Walt Disney arrived in Hollywood in the **1920s**, Pacific Electric Railway's Red Car Trolleys were part of the **largest** electrical railway system in the world. Over **1,000** miles of tracks and overhead electrical wires covered almost every nook and cranny of Los Angeles! Many people did not have their own car and hopped on these **handy trolleys** to get them wherever they needed to go. Today, you can ride on a replica of these famous **Red Cars** as they travel from Buena Vista Street to Hollywood Land and back again. If you catch a ride on a trolley—or see one passing by—look to see what **number** it has on it. Trolley **623** was given that number in honor of the year **1923** when Walt Disney moved to Los Angeles and the Pacific Electric Railway's 600 series of trolleys that it's modeled after. Trolley **717** is modeled after the 700 series of trolleys and was given that number in honor of **July 17, 1955**—the date of Disneyland's Opening Day!

SPY — Inside the trolley, take a look at the fun **advertisements** for things to do and see in DCA and beyond.

Photographs by Dave DeCaro • http://davelandweb.com | Red Car Trolley Illustration by | Shari Ewing • www.shariewingart.com

"We keep moving forward, opening new doors and doing new things, because we're curious, and curiosity keeps leading us down new paths."
—WALT DISNEY

FUN FACT

There's a private club in the Carthay Circle Restaurant building! Named for the year Walt Disney was born, Club 1901 is for members only.

SWANKY!

 ★ Food & Drinks

Carthay Circle Restaurant

This dazzling restaurant's rich wood paneling, floor-to-ceiling drapes and velvet benches set the stage for an elegant affair. Choose to sit in the main dining room, on the open-air terraces or—for a cozier setting—in one of the smaller rooms along the side which hold only one table each.

• *Seasonal cuisine featuring local meats, seafood & vegetables*

 **SPY** Don't miss the restaurants' incredible **ceiling** with scenes inspired by *Snow White and the Seven Dwarfs*.

Carthay Circle Lounge

Located on the ground floor below Carthay Circle Restaurant, this luxurious lounge is a stylish spot to take a break and enjoy some refreshments—or wait for your table to be ready upstairs.

• *Desserts* • *Small plates* • *Snacks*

Gone But not Forgotten

The design of Carthay Circle Restaurant was inspired by a real-life 1926 Hollywood landmark, **Carthay Circle Theatre.** Named after a version of its developer's last name: "McCarthy," this glitzy **movie palace** was known for its circular auditorium. The theater hosted the **glamorous premiere** of *Snow White and the Seven Dwarfs* in 1937 but was **torn down** in 1969. Thanks to Carthay Circle Restaurant, its **legacy** lives on in DCA.

 SPY Check out the **historical photos** on display in Carthay Circle Restaurant and Lounge.

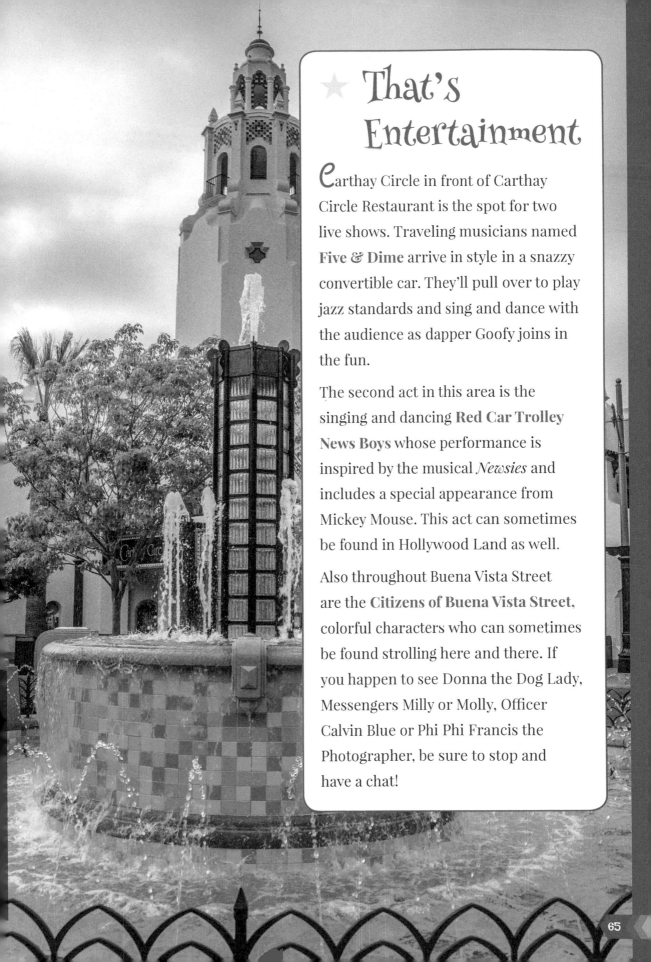

That's Entertainment

Carthay Circle in front of Carthay Circle Restaurant is the spot for two live shows. Traveling musicians named **Five & Dime** arrive in style in a snazzy convertible car. They'll pull over to play jazz standards and sing and dance with the audience as dapper Goofy joins in the fun.

The second act in this area is the singing and dancing **Red Car Trolley News Boys** whose performance is inspired by the musical *Newsies* and includes a special appearance from Mickey Mouse. This act can sometimes be found in Hollywood Land as well.

Also throughout Buena Vista Street are the **Citizens of Buena Vista Street**, colorful characters who can sometimes be found strolling here and there. If you happen to see Donna the Dog Lady, Messengers Milly or Molly, Officer Calvin Blue or Phi Phi Francis the Photographer, be sure to stop and have a chat!

65

CLARABELLE'S HAND-SCOOPED ICE CREAM

This charming ice cream parlor shares its name with Minnie Mouse's friend Clarabelle the Cow and features stained glass windows, pretty pastel tiles and scrolling ironwork. A play on the phrase "everything but the kitchen sink," you can actually get a sundae in a souvenir sink that's shaped like Mickey Mouse's famous red shorts! Another unique item on the menu is an ice cream bar that you customize yourself by deciding the flavor of the ice cream, the type of chocolate coating, and the topping you want—or if you want ALL of the toppings!

• *Ice cream cones* • *Strawberry sundae* • *The Oswald sundae*

HOT TIP Clarabelle's doesn't have any seating but it's **totally okay** to take your treats next door to the tables at **Fiddler, Fifer & Practical Café**.

SPY **Cone shapes** are all around Clarabelle's. Look at the windows, lighting and signs to see **how many** you can find.

FiDDLeR, FifeR & PRacticaL café

Look around this cozy coffee shop and you can't miss the photos and memorabilia from the singing trio The Silver Lake Sisters, who are known professionally as Fiddler, Fifer and Practical. Just like the pigs in Disney's popular Silly Symphony cartoons, Fiddler plays the violin, Fifer plays the flute and Practical plays the piano.

• *Pastries* • *Salads* • *Sandwiches*

SPY Look on the **bulletin board** inside the café to find an ad for **Piano Lessons** with Roger Radcliff. Roger is Pongo's owner in *101 Dalmatians* and a talented piano player.

The Disneyland Monorail passes through DCA on this bridge but only has stations in Downtown Disney and Disneyland!

MORTIMER'S MARKET

This grab-n-go corner market offers fresh and healthy options. The name Mortimer actually goes way back in Disney history. The legend goes that in the 1920s, Walt Disney wanted to name his new mouse character Mortimer but his wife Lillian suggested Mickey instead. In later Disney cartoons and comic strips there was a Mortimer Mouse, a not-so-nice character who tried to steal Minnie away from her main mouse.

• *Fruit* • *Ice-cold drinks* • *Veggies*

STORY TIME

Standing across from the fountain in Carthay Circle is the Storytellers statue. This bronze statue shows Walt Disney as he looked in his 20s when he arrived on the Santa Fe California Limited train from Kansas with nothing but a suitcase and a dream. Standing with him is his faithful pal, Mickey Mouse, excited to start on their new adventure together.

 Unlike many statues, this one is placed **right on the ground** so you can stand next to it, see how **tall** Walt was in real life and take an up-close photo.

 The design on the front of the **suitcase** looks like Walt Disney's **business card**.

★ Sample Souvenirs

Artistic Apple

The handmade caramel apples in **Trolley Treats** are so well-made, they're practically works of art. Crisp apples are dipped in caramel, coated in chocolate and then decorated in various holiday and character themes. This souvenir won't last long but a super-cute photo of you holding it will!

Conductor Cap

All aboard for railroad and trolley-themed goods at **Los Feliz Five & Dime** including this snazzy hat like a trolley conductor would wear—only with Mickey Mouse ears!

 HOT TIP Unlike many mouse ear hats, this one **CAN'T** be embroidered with your name on the back.

Oswald Ear Hat

Feeling lucky? Hop over to **Oswald's** to pick up your very own set of ta-a-a-a-ll ears to look just like your favorite lucky rabbit.

Mini Quiz!

Can you guess who invented caramel apples?
Answer on page 182.
- ☐ Dan Walker
- ☐ Daniel Colter
- ☐ Dapper Dan

Nine Old Men & One Special Young Lady

On the side of the Atwater Ink & Paint shop is a sign for the **Atwater School of Art & Animation** with a list of instructors. These names are a nod to the famous "Nine Old Men"—the playful nickname Walt gave to his top animators even though they were all young at the time. **Les Clark, Eric Larson, Ollie Johnston, Frank Thomas, Ward Kimball, Marc Davis, Milt Kahl, John Lounsbery** and **Wolfgang Reitherman** were all named Disney Legends in 1989. **The Atwater Ink & Paint shop** is named **"Atwater"** after Atwater Village where the animators hung out while working nearby at the Walt Disney Studios, and **"Ink & Paint"** after the studio's Ink and Paint Department. Ink and Paint artists traced drawings onto animation cels with ink, flipped them over and filled them in with paint. One of the most notable Ink and Paint artists was **Lillian Bounds** who ended up marrying none other than Walt Disney himself.

WHO SHOPS WHERE?

Which Disney character might shop in which of these **fake stores**?
Draw a line to connect the character's **name** with their
shopping bag. The first one's been
done for you. *Answers on page 182.*

Carl Fredricksen

Edna

Elsa

Goofy

Mickey Mouse

Mike Wazowski

The Beast

Ursula

Woody

SepulvedaBldg.

LESSING
KAMEN
and
JAMES
Counselors
Law

This building is named after Sepulveda Boulevard which, at almost 43 miles long, is the longest street in Los Angeles county.

HOLLYWOOD LAND

What Will You Find in This Chapter?

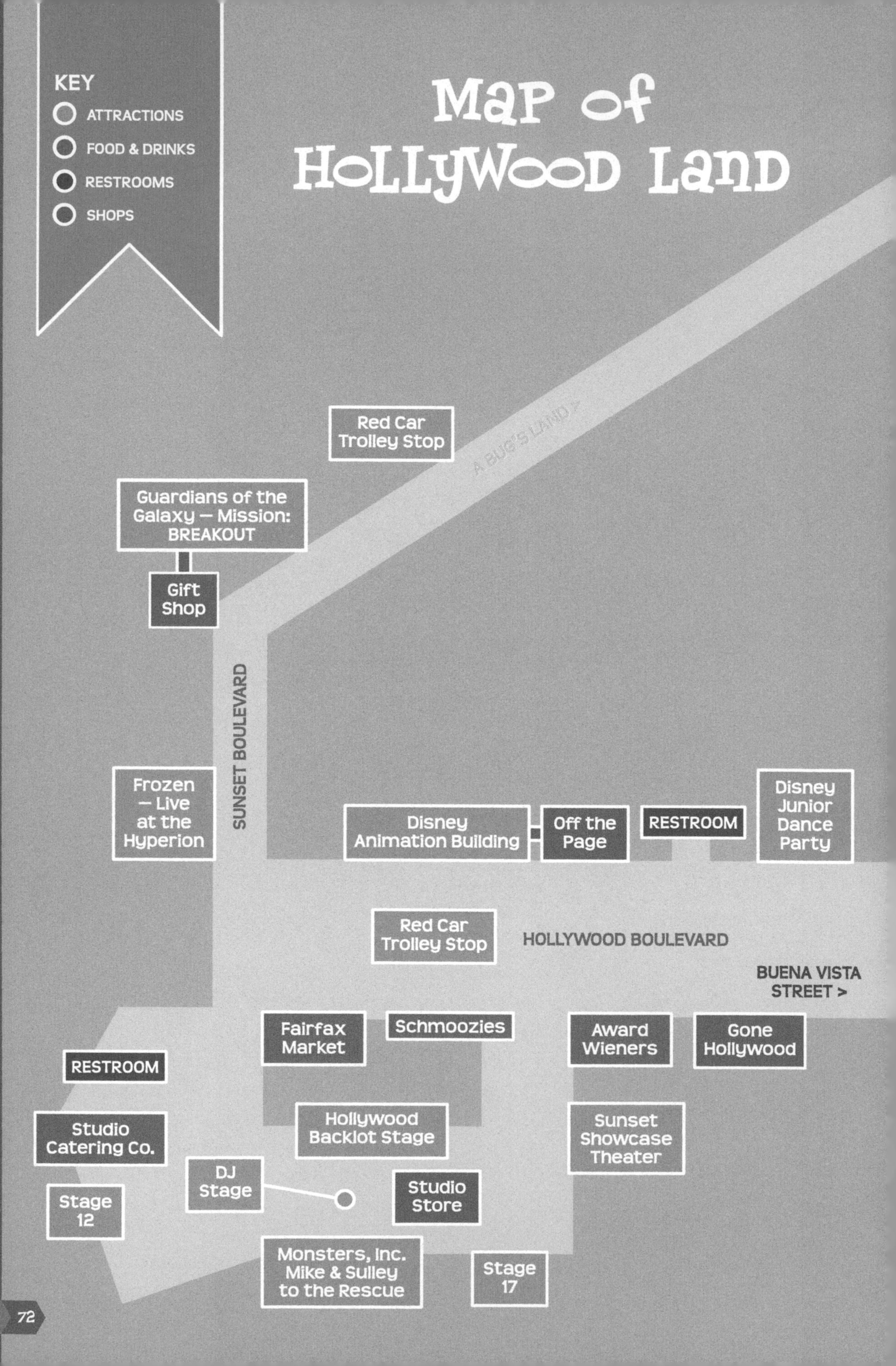

KEY
ATTRACTIONS
FOOD & DRINKS
RESTROOMS
SHOPS
MAP of HOLLYWOOD LAND
Red Car Trolley Stop
A BUG'S LAND >
Guardians of the Galaxy — Mission: BREAKOUT
Gift Shop
SUNSET BOULEVARD
Frozen — Live at the Hyperion
Disney Animation Building
Off the Page
RESTROOM
Disney Junior Dance Party
Red Car Trolley Stop
HOLLYWOOD BOULEVARD
BUENA VISTA STREET >
Fairfax Market
Schmoozies
Award Wieners
Gone Hollywood
RESTROOM
Studio Catering Co.
Hollywood Backlot Stage
Sunset Showcase Theater
DJ Stage
Studio Store
Stage 12
Monsters, Inc. Mike & Sulley to the Rescue
Stage 17

Lights! Camera! Action!

Back in the 1920s, a part of Los Angeles called Hollywood was becoming the center of the glamorous new movie industry. People came from all over America and beyond to try to make it big in Tinseltown. Imagine yourself back in the Golden Age of Hollywood when you explore Hollywood Land. Many of the buildings take their inspiration directly from historic landmarks in Hollywood, which is about 30 miles away from the Disneyland Resort. Home to almost all of the theaters in the park, this entertaining land celebrates the exciting history of Hollywood.

SPY

At the end of **Hollywood Boulevard,** notice how the backdrop makes the street seem to go into the distance. When the sky is **just the right shade of blue,** it's hard to tell where the painting ends and the sky begins!

I'D RATHER BE THE CAP!

Waiting Game!

WOULD YOU RATHER...
In this game for 2 players, ask the other player about whether they'd rather do **this** or **that.** For example, you could ask "Would you rather be Captain America or Spider-Man?" Then, ask them another "Would you rather..." question using the answer they picked and a new choice. After several rounds the other player may keep picking the same answer over and over. That means you have found what they would rather do more than anything else and the game is over and it's your turn to answer the "Would you rather..." questions.

★ Hollywood Land Venues

SO YOU KNOW...
venue = location where events takes place

DJ Stage & Hollywood Backlot Stage

These outdoor stages host various short-term events like ElecTRONica, Freeze the Night, Jammin' on the Backlot and Mad T Party.

Stage 12 & Stage 17

These large indoor spaces host special events like Annual Passholder events, the Food & Wine Festival and wedding receptions.

Sunset Showcase Theater

This theater shows sneak peeks of upcoming Disney movies.

★ That's Entertainment

Starting in Hollywood Land and ending in Paradise Pier, the **Pixar Play Parade** features fabulous floats, puppets, dancers & popular Disney•Pixar characters. Five, four, three, two, FUN!

Illustration by Lindsay Gibson • www.etsy.com/shop/emandsprout

THE WRIGHT RESTROOM

Hollywood Land has a **unique restroom** that was designed to look like Frank Lloyd Wright's famous Mayan Revival-style **Storer House**. Wright lived from 1867–1959 and is America's most famous **architect**—a person who designs how buildings will look. Storer House in Los Angeles was the **first structure** to use Wright's **textile block system** where concrete blocks were stacked to form walls. The house was built in 1923 and was named a **Historic-Cultural Landmark** in 1972. Today, the house still stands in the Hollywood Hills and recently sold for over **six-million bucks**.

Photograph by Dave DeCaro • http://daveland.web.com

Disney Junior Dance Party

INDOOR LIVE SHOW ★ EST. 2003 ★ Lively & Exciting

Put on your dancing shoes! Fans of Disney Junior won't want to miss this exciting live show at the Disney Theater. This interactive concert makes YOU a part of the high-energy fun as you sing and dance along with the action. You'll have a blast with friendly characters from popular Disney Junior shows like *Doc McStuffins*, *Sofia the First* and *The Lion Guard*. Beloved classic characters like Mickey and Minnie Mouse—who star in Disney Junior's *Mickey and the Roadster Racers*—join in the party too!

FUN FACT
Kion from "The Lion Guard" is the son of Simba from "The Lion King."

Who is your favorite Disney Junior character?

_____

TIME MACHINE

2001
DCA opens with ABC Soap Opera Bistro where Guests were part of daytime TV-style drama while they dined.

2003
Playhouse Disney – Live on Stage debuts at the new Disney Theater where ABC Soap Opera Bistro used to be.

2011
Playhouse Disney – Live on Stage changes to Disney Junior – Live on Stage with new characters & stories.

2017
Let's Dance! Disney Junior – Live on Stage changes to Disney Junior Dance Party.

FUN FACT

Monsters, Inc. Mike & Sulley to the Rescue is the ONLY ride in DCA that offers a Buddy Pass. Ask a Cast Member at the entrance if they're handing them out. If so, you & a friend can go in the exit & fill in a taxi that needs more riders.

COOL!

★ Monsters, Inc. Mike & Sulley to the Rescue

Where do monsters live? Monstropolis! And whether they are giant or tiny, furry or scaly, there's one thing that's always **terrified** them—humans! Hop in a taxi at the Monstropolis Transit Terminal and travel through the monsters' colorful city as a **2319** is in progress—the code for a human child being on the loose. Monsters Mike and Sulley know the little girl **Boo** is harmless and try to get her back home—though the sneaky monster **Randall** has other ideas. You'll pass through Harryhausen's Sushi Restaurant where the sight of Boo has caused a **panic** to break loose. As agents from the **CDA** (Child Detection Agency) spring into action, you'll head to the Monsters, Inc. factory with Randall in hot pursuit. After a chase scene in the **Door Vault** where door after door zips and zooms by, Mike and Sulley finally find Boo's **flowered door** and get her back home where she belongs.

INDOOR DARK RIDE — est. 2006 — Lively & Exciting

HOT TIP — There are actually special **smells** in this ride. See if you can pick up the scent of **ginger** in the sushi restaurant, **odorant** in the locker room and **lemon** snow cones in the Door Vault.

SPY — Look for **Roz** at the end of this ride. She's **"always watching"** Mike but now she's watching **YOU** and just might have something to say to you.

TIME MACHINE

2001
Superstar Limo is an Opening Day attraction where the Monsters, Inc. ride is now. It closes less than a year later.

2001
The world meets Mike Wazowski, James P. "Sulley" Sullivan & Boo when "Monsters, Inc." roars into theaters.

2006
Monsters, Inc. Mike & Sulley to the Rescue opens in DCA with a blue fur carpet premiere. How furbulous!

2013
"Monsters, Inc." gets a prequel when "Monsters University" hits theaters.

SPEAKING PIG LATIN!

In *Monsters, Inc.* Sulley tells Mike to "Ook-lay in the ag-bay"
which is Pig Latin for "Look in the bag." How does Pig Latin work?
You take the first letter or sound off the front of a word,
add it to the end and then add "ay" after that. If the word starts
with a vowel (A, E, I, O, U) just add "ay" at the end. For small words like
"in" "an" "or" and "the," you can leave them as is. Can you translate
this sentence from Pig Latin to English? *Answer on page 182.*

**"I an't-cay ait-way to ide-ray onsters-may
inc-ay ike-may and-ay ully-say to the escue-ray!"**

FUN FACT

Sorcerer's Workshop gets its name from the setting in "The Sorcerer's Apprentice" starring Mickey Mouse, part of the 1940 movie "Fantasia."

TA-DA!

★ Disney Animation Building

Interactive Exhibits ★ est. 2001 ★ Calm & Mellow

$\mathcal{A}$s you enter this cool building, the first area you'll come to is a **massive** lobby called Animation Courtyard which has huge screens covering its walls. This is a peaceful place to relax and view classic clips and artists' sketches from various animated Disney movies. Surrounding the lobby are separate areas you can explore to enjoy different experiences—which one will you check out first?

 HOT TIP Ursula's Grotto closed to make room for **Anna & Elsa's Royal Welcome** but may return in the future.

animation academy

Art school is in session! You'll take a seat in a large theater and get your own drawing board, pencil and paper to use during the class. Next, an artist on stage will lead you through a fun and easy step-by-step Disney character drawing lesson. People who think they can't draw will discover it's easier than they realize. Be sure to check the schedule to see which classes are being taught that day and at what time.

 HOT TIP The paper you'll get at Animation Academy has **"Disney Animation Academy"** printed on it, so your fabulous, incredible, absolutely stunning artwork makes a wonderful **free souvenir.**

 SPY Animation Academy's stage is designed to look like an **animator's studio** with a Sketch Desk and shelves filled with memorabilia.

★ Meet n' Greets

$\mathcal{E}$njoy a warm reception from Anna and Elsa at Anna & Elsa's Royal Welcome inside Disney Animation Building.

SORCERER'S WORKSHOP

SO YOU KNOW...
zoetrope = spinning device that gives the illusion of motion

The first section of Sorcerer's Workshop is a castle chamber called **Magic Mirror Realm** with the Evil Queen's magic mirror, colorful glowing lanterns and special drawing paper for creating simple animations. Once you're done with your drawing (which you can keep), load it into a **zoetrope** to see your doodles come to life. Next, wind through a dimly lit passage to visit the **Beast's Library** from *Beauty and the Beast* where you'll find a fireplace with the Prince's portrait hanging over the mantle and several desks dotted around the room. Take a seat and answer questions in an enchanted book to learn which character you are most like!

SPY Notice how the **lighting** and **mood** in the library changes. As you hear Belle saying **"I love you"** to the Beast, the last petal falls from the red rose on the mantle and the **dark spell** that has fallen over the library is broken.

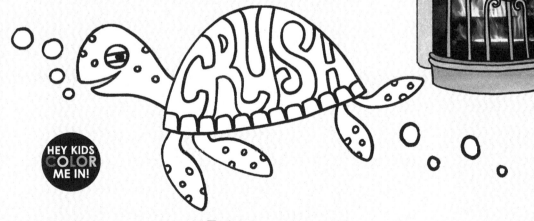

HEY KIDS COLOR ME IN!

TURTLE TALK WITH CRUSH

Du-u-u-de, no way! In this interactive show you can get up close and personal with Crush the Turtle and other characters from *Finding Nemo* and *Finding Dory*. A Cast Member will get the show started and help the audience call out for Crush to swim into view in the "Window to the Pacific" in the front of the theater. Crush will chat with the audience, asking and answering questions, and teaching his human friends how to talk turtle. No two shows are the same so you might want to drop in more than once.

HOT TIP If **you** want to try to talk with Crush, find a seat in the **front** or beside the **aisles** so the Cast Member will have a better chance of reaching you with their **microphone.**

FUN FACT

Guests to Hyperion Theater are surrounded by an enormous "Aurora" curtain which features special lighting & projected images as part of the show.

FANCY!

Read the Super, Super-Short Story of "Frozen" and other tales on page 177!

Photograph by Dave DeCaro • http://davelandweb.com

★ # Frozen – Live at the Hyperion

LIVE STAGE SHOW
—est.—
2016
Lively & exciting

Enjoy a unique retelling of everyone's favorite frosty flick at this (almost) 2,000-seat theater. This live musical stage show features gorgeous costumes, elaborate sets, incredible special effects and clever puppetry. The story unfolds in front of an enormous video wall as all of your favorite *Frozen* characters tell the epic tale of Princess Anna and Queen Elsa of Arendelle and the magical power of true love.

TIME MACHINE

2001	2003	2013	2016
Hyperion Theater is an Opening Day Attraction in DCA with "Steps In Time" as its first show.	*Disney's Aladdin: A Musical Spectacular opens at Hyperion Theater & plays for 13 years.*	*"Frozen" frenzy begins when "Frozen" hits theaters.*	*Frozen – Live at the Hyperion makes its debut. Let's all go, let's all go!*

"Do you wanna build a snowman?"
—ANNA

"What should we do next—something good, something bad? Bit of both?"
—PETER QUILL

FUN FACT

The Collector's Fortress stands at 183 feet & is not only the tallest structure in the Disneyland Resort but also one of the tallest buildings in the entire city of Anaheim.

GOLLY!

★ Guardians of the Galaxy – Mission: BREAKOUT

INDOOR DROP TOWER ★ WILD & THRILLING ★ —EST.— 2017

Are you ready to brave the unknown in an alien fortress? Enter the lair of Taneleer Tivan, otherwise known as The Collector. Taneleer's life's work has been to gather living beings and artifacts from hundreds of thousands of planets all over the known universe. His strange and unusual museum looms above the treetops and is powered by a massive generator that keeps his rare possessions safe and secure. After walking through the Gardens of the Galaxy, you'll marvel at The Collector's vast array of oddities including his newest treasures—the Guardians of the Galaxy, held captive in glass cases! When Rocket Racoon escapes from his case, he'll enlist your help to free the rest of the crew. As a song from Peter Quill's awesome mixtape plays, you'll plummet toward the ground in a gantry lift elevator and back up again in a freefall adventure!

HOT TIP

As you scream up and down the **gantry shaft**, your photo will be taken and you can buy a copy in the **gift shop** on the way out.

TIME MACHINE

1959
"The Twilight Zone" TV series first airs & runs until 1964.

2004
The Twilight Zone Tower of Terror opens in Disney California Adventure. Yikes!

2014
"Guardians of the Galaxy" hits theaters.

2017
The Twilight Zone Tower of Terror transforms into Guardians of the Galaxy – Mission: BREAKOUT.

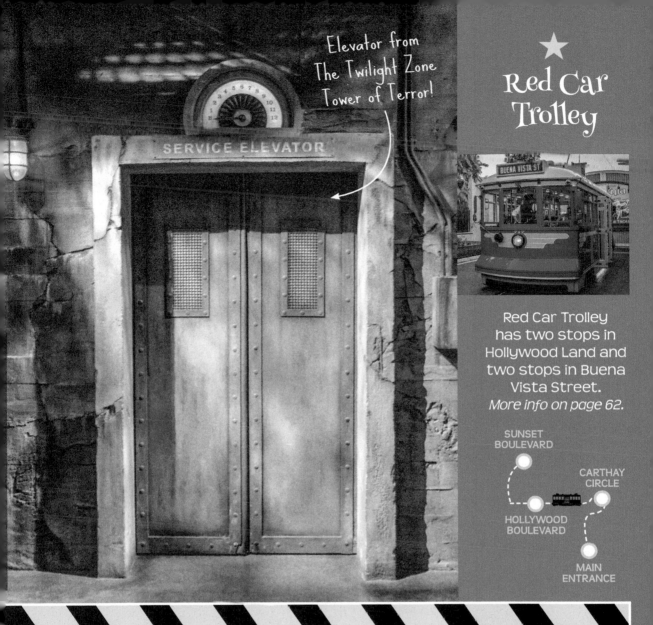

Elevator from The Twilight Zone Tower of Terror!

SERVICE ELEVATOR

★ Red Car Trolley

Red Car Trolley has two stops in Hollywood Land and two stops in Buena Vista Street.
More info on page 62.

SUNSET BOULEVARD

CARTHAY CIRCLE

HOLLYWOOD BOULEVARD

MAIN ENTRANCE

Imagineers at Play

In the summer of 2016, Imagineers announced that **The Twilight Zone Tower of Terror** would close and reopen in 2017 with a *Guardians of the Galaxy* theme. These popular movies—with **awesome** soundtracks—feature the adventures of Peter Quill (A.K.A. Star-Lord) and a band of loveable misfits, including Rocket Racoon, Groot, Gamora and Drax the Destroyer. Though the attraction is completely **reimagined**, the **ride mechanism** is the same. In the original version, Guests entered the **Hollywood Tower Hotel** and traveled **through another dimension** to relive a stormy night when lightning struck a hotel **elevator** and the people inside of it **disappeared!**

DID YOU EAT IN HOLLYWOOD LAND?

☐ Yes ☐ No

If yes, where?

_____

What'd ya have?

_____

_____

_____

Was it good?

☐ Yes ☐ No
☐ Maybe So

FUN FACT

Originally, the hilltop "Hollywood" sign said "Hollywoodland" to advertise a 1923 housing development. About 20 years later, the "land" part was removed. Today, the sign is a famous symbol of this unique city.

HOORAY!

HOLLYWOOD

★ Food & Drinks

 HOT TIP Hollywood Land's eateries are all **on-the-go** style but you can find **outdoor seating areas** near Studio Catering Co. and Sunset Showcase Theater.

AWARD WIENERS

A play on the phrase "award winners" which is often heard in Hollywood, this sleek chrome and neon-lined trolley car serves up a variety of hot dogs and sausages.
• *Barbecue hot link sausages* • *Chili cheese dogs* • *Hot dog combo*

FAIRFAX MARKET

Named after the Fairfax District in Los Angeles, this sidewalk market specializes in fresh, healthy options.
• *Chips* • *Fruit* • *Pickles*

SCHMOOZIES

Schmooze over smoothies at Schmoozies! This spot for specialty drinks is made to look like one of the buildings at the Hollywood landmark Crossroads of the World on Sunset Boulevard.
• *Juice*
• *Smoothies*
• *Specialty coffee drinks*

SO YOU KNOW...
schmooze = chat with someone, often to try and get them to do something you want

STUDIO CATERING CO.

Enjoy snacks from this food truck parked near Stage 12 and the Hollywood Backlot Stage.
• *Chips* • *Frozen slush* • *Tot-chos*

Cap

★ Meet n' Greets

Swing by to meet Captain America and Spider-Man hanging out across from Studio Catering Co.

Spidey

aWaRD WinneRS!

And the Oscar goes to...**Walt Disney!** An Academy Award is the movie industry's highest honor. The winner is given a golden, man-shaped statue called an **Oscar.** Walt Disney holds the record for the most Academy Awards given to any individual in history—**twenty-six!** His first win was for the Silly Symphony cartoon *Flowers and Trees* in 1932. When Walt was given an **honorary Oscar** for *Snow White and the Seven Dwarfs,* the statue was custom-made to have **one** regular-sized figure with **seven** smaller ones to represent the dwarfs! During Walt's lifetime and after, The Walt Disney Company's movies have won **many** Academy Awards—especially the Best Song award. Can you name the movies that featured the **Oscar-winning songs** below: *Aladdin, Beauty and the Beast, Frozen, Mary Poppins, Monsters, Inc., Pinocchio, Pocahontas, The Little Mermaid, Tarzan* or *The Lion King.* The first one's been done for you. *Answers on page 182.*

"If we have any of these statues left over, we'll just send them to Walt Disney."
—BOB HOPE

FUN FaCT
The Academy of Motion Picture Arts & Sciences give out the Academy Awards. Rumor has it that an Academy employee thought that the award statues looked like her Uncle Oscar so the staff began calling them "Oscars."

AH HA!

| A Whole New World | Beauty and the Beast |
Aladdin	

Can You Feel the Love Tonight	Chim Chim Cher-ee

Colors of the Wind	If I Didn't Have You

Let It Go	Under the Sea

When You Wish Upon a Star	You'll Be in My Heart

The Absolutely Epic Eye Spy Game!

You'll find these mosaic tile walls at **Schmoozies** in Hollywood Land.
See if you can spy the items listed on the **opposite page** in the photos.
There are **more than one** of some of the objects. **Happy hunting!**

SPY

☐ Bananas	☐ Eyeglasses	☐ Horse	☐ Rainbow
☐ Bee	☐ Flowered mug	☐ Hummingbird	☐ Sailboat
☐ Cat in a shoe	☐ Fork	☐ Measuring cup	☐ Swan
☐ Duck's head	☐ Frog	☐ Musical note	☐ Toy car

★ Sample Souvenirs

FROZEN BRACELET

There are a few different places around the Disneyland Resort to get a personalized leather bracelet but the **cart near Hyperion Theater** is the only spot where you'll find *Frozen*-themed metallic leather. Choose your style, color, lettering and if you want to add extra decorative doodads.

ORIGINAL SKETCH

Ever wish you could own an original drawing by a real Disney artist? Your wish can come true at **Off the Page**. Head over to the Sketch Desk and choose from the finished character sketches or chat with the artist about a custom order.

SPY Even if an **original drawing** isn't in your budget, it's lots of fun to **watch** the artists.

DISNEY LEGEND CLOSE-UP: ALAN MENKEN

Alan Menken is a musician and a songwriter but he's most famous for being a **composer**—someone who writes the **music** for a song. Alan has written the music for **many** beloved Disney songs. Growing up in New York, Alan took piano and violin lessons but was bored playing the songs he was supposed to practice and started making up his own! After graduating from **New York University** with a degree in musicology, he wrote a rock ballet. The best part about that was he met and fell in love with a **beautiful ballerina** who became his wife. Soon after that, Alan teamed up with Howard Ashman who was a talented **lyricist**—someone who writes the **words** for a song. The two created an off-Broadway musical called *Little Shop of Horrors*. The show was **such a hit** that The Walt Disney Company hired them to write the music and lyrics for *The Little Mermaid*. This movie—and its music—made a **huge splash** and marked a new chapter for Disney animation. Alan went on to write the music for *Aladdin, Beauty and the Beast, Enchanted, Hercules, Newsies, Pocahontas, Tangled* and *The Hunchback of Notre Dame*. Alan was named a Disney Legend in 2001.

Costume Call!

The **Costume Department** is an important part of a Hollywood movie production. Costume designers create outfits for actors to wear, just like storyboard artists and animators create outfits for animated characters. Write the **character's name** on the tag attached to their **vest**: Aladdin, Fear, Flynn Rider, Goofy, Judy Hopps, Pinocchio, Snow White's Prince, White Rabbit or Woody. The first one's been done for you. *Answers on page 182.*

White Rabbit

This building is like a movie set where
only the front of the building is finished.

a BUG'S LanD

What Will You Find in This Chapter?

ATTRACTIONS
- Flik's Flyers
- Francis' Ladybug Boogie
- Heimlich's Chew Chew Train
- Tuck and Roll's Drive 'Em Buggies

ENTERTAINMENT
- It's Tough to be a Bug

ACTIVITIES, GAMES & INFO
- A Bug's Life Primer
- It's All in the Details!
- Puddle Play
- Say What? Disney•Pixar Edition!

KEY

- ATTRACTIONS
- RESTROOMS

CARS LAND >

Tuck & Roll's Drive 'Em Buggies

Heimlich's Chew Chew Train

^
PACIFIC WHARF

^
CARS LAND

FLIK'S FUN FAIR

Francis' Ladybug Boogie

Princess Dot Puddle Park

It's Tough to be a Bug

RESTROOM

< HOLLYWOOD LAND

< BUENA VISTA STREET

Flik's Flyers

It's Fun to be a Bug!

Look at the world through the eyes of a bug when you enter this lush, leafy land inspired by Disney•Pixar's *A Bug's Life*. In this whimsical area, you can scamper through a cereal box, relax on a bench made of popsicle sticks and frolic under a garden hose. Flik the Ant is famous for his clever inventions and has put together a Fun Fair of cute carnival rides and a splash pad crafted from discarded objects. Overhead, towering plants and clovers create a shady, green oasis as humming and chirping insect sounds fill the air.

 A Bug's Land has **no shops or restaurants** but there are **snack carts** if you need a little something and don't want to hop over to another land.

 See if you can find the giant **lucky clover** somewhere in A Bug's Land that has **four** leaves instead of **three**!

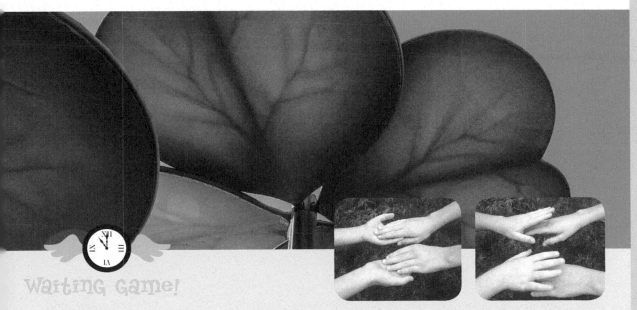

Waiting Game!

SWAT THE BUG

In this game for 2 players, start by putting both of your hands out, palms up. The other player is The Bug and rests their hands on top of yours, palms down. As you try to quickly flip your hands over to swat The Bug, the other person quickly tries to pull their hands away. If they move their hands away before you can touch them, they win. If you are able to touch them in time, you win.

a BUG'S Life PRimeR

NAME Dim
TYPE OF BUG
Rhinoceros Beetle
QUOTE *"Roar-rrrrrrrrrrr!"*
WHAT MAKES HIM TICK
Being the lion in the lion-taming act in P.T. Flea's Circus
PERSONALITY Childlike, ticklish, protective

NAME Flik
TYPE OF BUG
Ant
QUOTE "We'll just use our imaginations."
WHAT MAKES HIM TICK
Trying to find an inventive way to save Ant Island from the grasshoppers
PERSONALITY Nerdy, clever, creative

NAME Francis
TYPE OF BUG
Ladybug
QUOTE "I heard that, you twig!"
WHAT MAKES ~~HER~~ HIM TICK
Making sure no one mistakes him for a lady & being a clown in P.T. Flea's Circus
PERSONALITY Grumpy, aggressive, short-tempered

NAME Gypsy
TYPE OF BUG
Gypsy Moth
QUOTE "The stage is the other way, dear."
WHAT MAKES HER TICK
Being Manny's wife & lovely assistant for the magic act in P.T. Flea's Circus
PERSONALITY Protective, kind-hearted, brave

NAME Heimlich
TYPE OF BUG
Caterpillar
QUOTE "Bottle all gone. Baby wants pie!"
WHAT MAKES HIM TICK
Dreaming of becoming a butterfly & being a clown in P.T. Flea's Circus
PERSONALITY Sweet, obsessed with food, daydreamer

NAME Hopper
TYPE OF BUG
Grasshopper
QUOTE "It's not about food, it's about keeping those ants in line."
WHAT MAKES HIM TICK
Ordering the ants of Ant Island to collect food for the grasshoppers
PERSONALITY Mean, bossy, demanding

NAME **Manny**
TYPE OF BUG
Praying Mantis
QUOTE "I've made a living out of being a failure & you, Sir, are not a failure."
WHAT MAKES HIM TICK
Being an underappreciated magician in P.T. Flea's Circus
PERSONALITY Dignified, kind, polite

NAME **P.T. Flea**
TYPE OF BUG
Flea
QUOTE "No refunds after the first two minutes."
WHAT MAKES HIM TICK
Being the ringmaster at his Flea Circus & bossing around his performers
PERSONALITY Greedy, cheap, opportunistic

NAME **Rosie**
TYPE OF BUG
Black Widow Spider
QUOTE "I mean, I've always been a black widow, but now I'm a black widow *widow.*"
WHAT MAKES HER TICK
Being the lion tamer in the lion-taming act in P.T. Flea's Circus
PERSONALITY Mother-like, friendly, husbandless

NAME **Slim**
TYPE OF BUG
Stick Insect
QUOTE "I am the only stick with eyeballs!"
WHAT MAKES HIM TICK
Being a clown in P.T. Flea's Circus
PERSONALITY Nervous, disgruntled, unpredictable

NAMES **The Queen, Princess Atta & Dot**
TYPE OF BUG
Ants
QUOTE "It's not a lot but it's our life."—The Queen
WHAT MAKES THEM TICK
Trying to do what's best for their colony on Ant Island
PERSONALITY Caring, responsible, good-hearted

NAMES **Tuck & Roll**
TYPE OF BUG
Pill Bugs
QUOTE "Hey!"—Roll
WHAT MAKES THEM TICK
Being the acrobatic act in P.T. Flea's Circus
PERSONALITY Enthusiastic, energetic, active

FUN FACT

Ants are amazing creatures. They can carry objects 50 times their own body weight. IF YOU had the strength of an ant, you'd be able to lift a small car over your head.

ANT POWER!

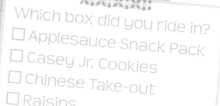

Which box did you ride in?
- ☐ Applesauce Snack Pack
- ☐ Casey Jr. Cookies
- ☐ Chinese Take-out
- ☐ Raisins

★ Flik's Flyers

est. 2002 — OUTDOOR SPINNING RIDE • Lively & exciting

Wouldn't you like to ride in Flik's beautiful balloon? Look closely and you'll see Flik's cute contraption is made from leaves sewn together, twigs and food boxes, with a base made from a whipped cream container and a pie plate. As gears clank, buzz and whir, your hot air balloon will lift from the ground and spin through the skies of A Bug's Land!

SPY

Some of the balloons have **Casey Jr. Cookie** boxes like the ones that made up **P.T. Flea's Circus Train** in *A Bug's Life*. This train was a nod to the **Casey Jr. Circus Train** in the 1941 movie *Dumbo and* the ride over in **Disneyland**. Try to find Casey Jr. Cookies **somewhere else** in A Bug's Land!

TIME MACHINE

1994
Disney•Pixar's story team dream up "A Bug's Life," "Finding Nemo," "Monsters, Inc." & "WALL•E" over a VERY productive lunch.

1998
Bug out! The Disney•Pixar movie "A Bug's Life" hits theaters.

2001
It's Tough to be a Bug is an Opening Day attraction in Disney California Adventure.

2002
A Bug's Land opens in DCA & includes the already existing theater & Flik's Fun Fair.

★ Francis' Ladybug Boogie

Francis gets very grouchy when someone mistakes him for a lady but you'll feel anything but grouchy when you hop in one of his spinning spotted ladybugs! You'll whip through a figure-eight path as the swinging "Ladybug Boogie" music fills the air.

★ Outdoor Spinning Ride ★ Lively & Exciting ★
est. 2002

SPY Look up to see **firefly lights** near this ride and all around A Bug's Land.

FUN FACT

Why does a ladybug have spots? The black-and-red pattern sends a message to predators: "Leave me alone, I taste awful!"

CLEVER!

"Who you callin' lady!?"
—FRANCIS

It's all in the Details!

The bugs have made **many** clever signs, lights, railings and more from objects they've found in the human world. Put a ✓ in the box next to the ones you see.

- ☐ Blue fork
- ☐ Number 2 pencil
- ☐ Pink drinking straw
- ☐ Purple crayon
- ☐ Christmas lights
- ☐ Paper airplane
- ☐ Popsicle stick
- ☐ Record

Hint! Hint!

FUN FACT

Pill bugs—who are also called roly poly bugs or potato bugs—will roll themselves into a ball when they think they're in danger, eat their own poop & can drink water with their mouth parts OR their rear end!

LOVELY!

★ Tuck and Roll's Drive 'Em Buggies

GENTLE BUMPER CARS
— EST. —
2002
Lively & exciting

Look for the Big Top tent made from a red-and-white umbrella and you've found P.T. Flea's Circus and this bumper car ride. Tuck (two eyebrows) and Roll (one eyebrow) are acrobatic pill bugs from Hungary who don't speak much English. As you drive your buggy, you'll hear them chattering about something— but just what they're saying is a mystery. You control where your buggy goes and if you want to bump into someone or try to stay clear. Each buggy has big rubber bumpers, so if you do have a collision you'll bounce right back.

HOT TIP A sign for this ride is a comb wrapped with paper. This is a musical instrument called a **comb kazoo!** Wrap a comb in waxed paper to make one at home.

Did you ride in a Tuck buggy (two eyebrows) or a Roll buggy (one eyebrow)?
□ Tuck □ Roll

HEY KIDS COLOR ME IN!

FUN FACT

A caterpillar has one job in life—to eat. Some can eat 27,000 times their own body weight in their lifetime.

CHOW DOWN!!

★ Heimlich's Chew Chew Train

★ CATERPILLAR TRAIN RIDE ★ CALM & MELLOW — est. — 2002

Burp! Heimlich the Caterpillar is delighted to give you a ride as he chew chews his way through a garden of tasty discarded delights. Always ready for a yummy snack, he'll chomp his way past carrots, a juicy apple and more as he chats cheerfully with you in his charming German accent. You'll wind under an arch made from a watermelon just before you reach a fork in the road. Will Heimlich turn right to head for Brussel Sprouts or left to visit Candy Valley?

"I have to eat lots of fruit if I want to grow up to become a beautiful butterfly."
—HEIMLICH

Butterfly

The Life of a Caterpillar

CHRYSALIS

EGGS

CATERPILLAR

HOT TIP
Pay close attention! As you ride this train you can actually smell some of the foods you're passing.

FUN FACT

*It's Tough to be a Bug
is named as a tribute to
an Oscar-winning Disney
short film called "It's
Tough to be a Bird."*

OH!

MAY BE
SCARY

★ # It's Tough To Be A Bug

INDOOR SHOW
★ —EST.— ★
2001
Lively & exciting

Scuttle underground and take a seat to enjoy a 3D movie hosted by friendly Flik. When he gives the word, you'll put on a special pair of bug eye glasses to become an honorary bug and see what life is like for them. The show is filled with surprises that you'll see—*and feel*. Thing get a little hairy when Hopper the Grasshopper tries to exterminate the audience but the show ends on an upbeat note with cheerful bees, dung beetles and dragonflies singing about how much bugs help our planet.

 HOT TIP Sometimes this venue is used for showing **sneak peeks** of upcoming Disney movies.

 SPY Before the show, take a look around the lobby at the **funny posters** for bug-themed musicals like *Beauty and the Bees* and *My Fair Ladybug*.

PUDDLE PLAY

Splash and play under a leaky garden hose in **Princess Dot Puddle Park!** Princess Dot is the adorable little daughter of the Queen of Ant Island. Her **splash pad** has fountains in the ground that spurt jets of water when you least expect it, so **get ready to get wet!**

 HOT TIP You can end up **quite soaked** here so you might want to bring an **extra outfit.** Head for the restroom made from an **upside-down tissue box** next to this play area to change out of your wet clothes.

say WHat? Disney·Pixar edition!

Guess **which** character said **what**. Draw a **speech bubble** from their name to their quote. The first one's been done for you. *Answers on page 182.*

So long, boys! I'll send you a postcard from Paradise Falls!

Carl Fredricksen

Dug

Edna Mode

Francis

Mrs. Potato Head

Roz

Wreck-It Ralph

Your stunned silence is very reassuring.

No capes!

I am bad and that's good. I will never be good and that's not bad.

I'm packing you an extra pair of shoes and your angry eyes —just in case.

I was hiding under your porch because I love you.

So, bein' a ladybug automatically makes me a girl. Is that it, flyboy?

You'll find bug statues like Manny the Praying Mantis all around A Bug's Land.

CARS LAND

What Will You Find in This Chapter?

ATTRACTIONS
- Luigi's Rollickin' Roadsters
- Mater's Junkyard Jamboree
- Radiator Springs Racers

ENTERTAINMENT
- DJ's Dance 'n' Drive

FOOD & DRINKS
- Cozy Cone Motel
- Fillmore's Taste-In
- Flo's V8 Café

MEET N' GREETS
- Lightning McQueen
- Mater
- Red the Fire Engine

SHOPS
- Lube-O-Rama
- Radiator Springs Curios
- Ramone's House of Body Art
- Sarge's Surplus Hut

ACTIVITIES, GAMES & INFO
- Cars Name Scrambles!
- Birth of the Billboard
- Motorama Girls Match-Up!
- Sample Souvenirs
- The Man Behind the Cars
- Bumper Sticker Bonanza!

Map of Cars Land

KEY

- ◯ ATTRACTIONS
- ◯ FOOD & DRINKS
- ◯ HELPFUL SPOTS
- ● RESTROOMS
- ◯ SHOPS

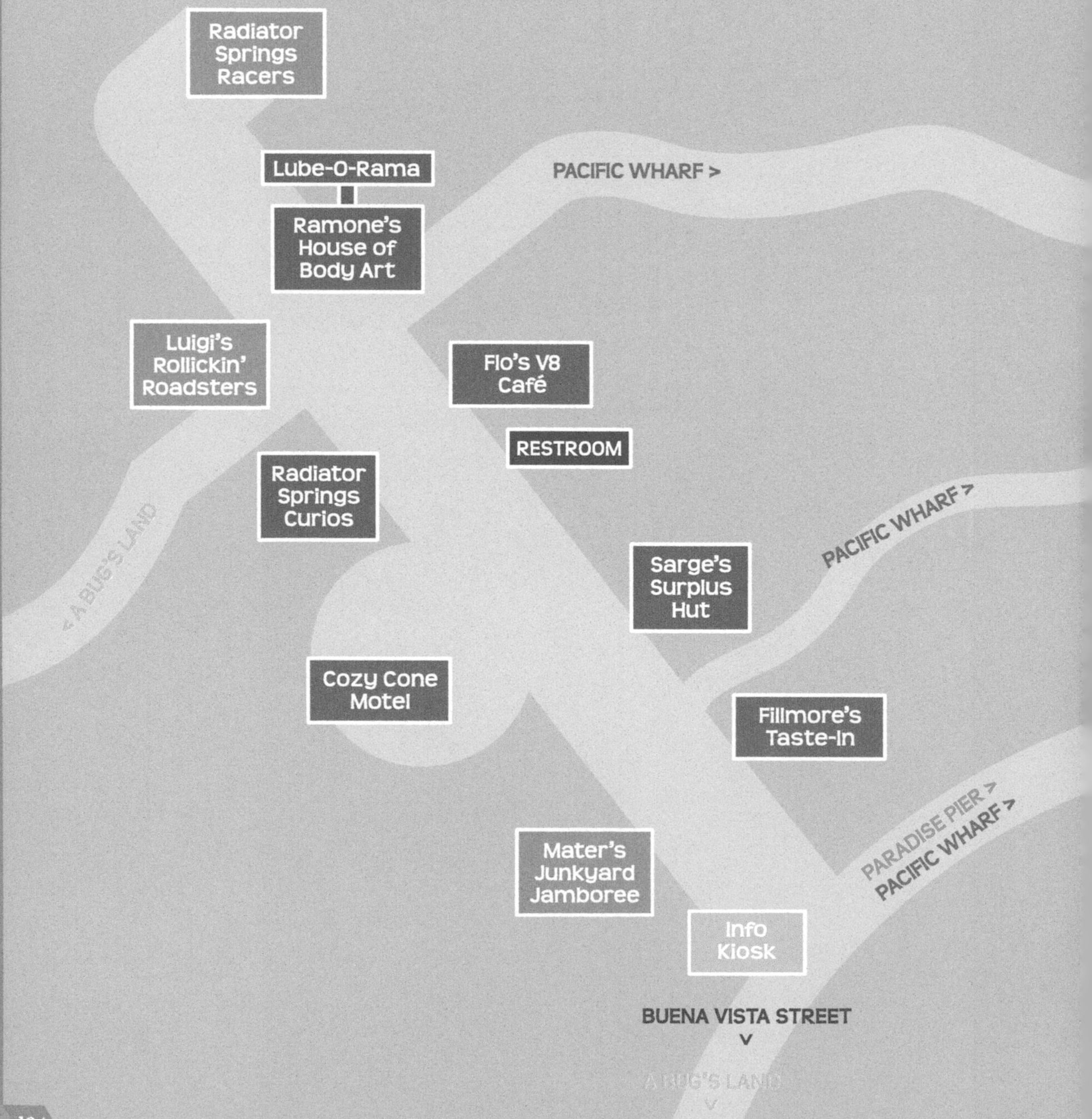

Radiator Springs Racers

Lube-O-Rama

PACIFIC WHARF >

Ramone's House of Body Art

Luigi's Rollickin' Roadsters

Flo's V8 Café

RESTROOM

< A BUG'S LAND

Radiator Springs Curios

PACIFIC WHARF >

Sarge's Surplus Hut

Cozy Cone Motel

Fillmore's Taste-In

PARADISE PIER >

PACIFIC WHARF >

Mater's Junkyard Jamboree

Info Kiosk

BUENA VISTA STREET
∨

A BUG'S LAND
∨

Start Your Engines!

Take a road trip through sights and sounds made famous in the *Cars* movies. Motor back to the glory days of Route 66 and experience the retro charm of Radiator Springs and Ornament Valley. From the classic roadside billboard sign to the awe-inspiring Cadillac Range mountains, there are so many special details in this land that you'll find lots to see and do before it's time to hit the road.

SPY Swing by Cars Land at sunset and stand in the road in front of **Flo's V8 Café** for a good view of Cars Land's **neon lights** coming on one by one as *Sh-Boom (Life Could Be a Dream)* plays.

WHAT COLOR WAS THE SEAT ON OUR LAST RIDE?

ORANGE!

Waiting Game!

OBSERVANT OBSERVER

Put the other people in your group to the test by asking them questions about things you've experienced together throughout the day. For example, you could ask "What was the number on the gate we walked through to enter the park?" or "What was the name of the Cast Member who helped us on Radiator Springs Racers?" Choose one person to ask the questions or take turns. Play just for fun or have players raise their hand to answer and win a point each time they are correct.

FUN FACT

A traditional square dance starts with four couples facing each other in a square. The dancers do the dance steps called out by a caller, like "California Twirl," "Promenade" & "Do-si-do."

YEEHAW!

★ Mater's Junkyard Jamboree

OUTDOOR SPINNING RIDE ★ LIVELY & EXCITING ★ — est. — 2012

Grab your tractor and do-si-do! Radiator Springs' resident hillbilly tow truck Tow Mater is hosting a square dance in his junkyard and the little tractors are having a swinging time. As the tractors dance and twirl, the trailer you're sitting in will whip from side to side. Nearby a jukebox made from discarded junk plays toe-tapping tunes performed by Mater and Billy Hill and the Hillbillies, a band who used to play in Disneyland's Golden Horseshoe restaurant.

 HOT TIP Every now and then, a **blooper song** plays where Mater sings **"dadgum...dadgum...dadgum"** because he can't remember the words.

 SPY Look closely at your tractor's **eye color, markings** and **facial expression**—no two are exactly alike!

Which one of Mater's songs do you like best?
- ☐ Big Bulldozer
- ☐ Let's Go Driving
- ☐ Junkyard Jamboree
- ☐ Mater's Square Dance
- ☐ Radiator Rock
- ☐ The One You Want To Call
- ☐ Welcome to Radiator Springs
- ☐ The Blooper Song

TIME MACHINE

2006
The world says "Howdy" to Tow Mater in the Disney•Pixar movie "Cars."

2011
Mater, Lightning McQueen & the rest of the gang are back in "Cars 2." Ka-chow!

2012
The baby tractors make their debut in DCA when Mater's Junkyard Jamboree opens as part of Cars Land.

2017
"Cars 3" hits theaters in the summer.

"I'm happier 'n a tornado in a trailer park! "
—MATER

CARS NAME SCRAMBLES!

Unscramble the names of these *Cars* characters.
The first one's been done for you. *Answers on page 182.*

GINGNIHTL QNEMEUC — Lightning McQueen	IGLIU
ERAMT	HCCIK CKHSI
CDO NDHSUO	MFEILRLO
LSLAY RRRCAEA	ZILEIZ
NEROAM	IGDUO

★ Meet n' Greets

Get up close and personal with Lightning McQueen or Mater when they pull up in front of Cozy Cone Motel—and other locations around Cars Land. Red the Fire Engine can often be found near Luigi's Rollickin' Roadsters.

FUN FACT

The Italian car company Fiat makes a type of car called a Topolino. This is not only the name of Luigi's uncle but also what Mickey Mouse is called in Italy.

CUTE!

★ Luigi's Rollickin' Roadsters

OUTDOOR CAR RIDE ★ est. 2016 ★ Lively & exciting

Surprise! You'll never know which way you're headed next on this **cute** and colorful ride. Luigi, the vintage Italian Fiat, runs a tire shop called **Casa Della Tires**—home to the Leaning Tower of Tires. In celebration of Race Day, he's invited his **cousins** from Carsoli to come and perform traditional dances in the yard behind his shop. Pick a convertible Italian roadster, hop in and **enjoy** as Luigi's family **whisks** you all around the dance floor in fun and lively formations.

HOT TIP
Each car has their own **signature dance move** and **unique style.** While waiting for your turn, pick out which car you want to try to ride.

SPY
Notice the **"autopiary"** bushes around the yard shaped like **tires** and Luigi's favorite race car, **Francesco Bernoulli.**

Ciao Sophia!

TIME MACHINE

1961
Disneyland's Flying Saucers opens & Guests steer themselves around on a cushion of air until the ride closes in 1966.

2012
Luigi's Flying Tires opens as part of Cars Land & uses the same concept as Disneyland's Flying Saucers.

2015
Luigi's Flying Tires closes to make way for a new attraction for Luigi.

2016
Luigi's Rollickin' Roadsters opens & is the Disneyland Resort's first trackless ride system. Andiamo!

Meet THE COUSINS FROM CARSOLI!

Luigi's Rollickin' Roadsters has **20 ride cars**—10 female and 10 male (with chrome grill mustaches). The cars have different eye colors, paint jobs, details and license plates. Put a ✔ next to the one(s) you ride on!

ANGELO ☐	CARINA ☐	CARLO ☐	CARLOTTA ☐
CARSOLI JK 0105	CARSOLI RM 0314	CARSOLI AS 2504	CARSOLI DK 0118

CARMELA ☐	ELISABETTA ☐	FRANCESCA ☐	GINA ☐
CARSOLI SB 3017	CARSOLI JC 0812	CARSOLI SW 0319	CARSOLI BD 0515

GIOVANNI ☐	ISABELLA ☐	LORENZO ☐	LUCIA ☐
CARSOLI BP 2503	CARSOLI JM 2220	CARSOLI MW 1802	CARSOLI DG 2716

NICCOLO ☐	PASQUALE ☐	ROSA ☐	SALVATORE ☐
CARSOLI PR 1113	CARSOLI JM 0707	CARSOLI SW 1206	CARSOLI NR 3001

SERGIO ☐	SOPHIA ☐	TONY ☐	VITO ☐
CARSOLI FM 2608	CARSOLI RW 3109	CARSOLI AA 1211	CARSOLI KR 0710

★ Radiator Springs Racers

Hop in a convertible car and motor off on a grand adventure. Though you'll be racing later, your trip starts off peacefully as you wind past a beautiful waterfall and the amazing red rock formations of Ornament Valley. Next, you'll head into a dark tunnel and narrowly miss some other cars and a train before Mater shows you his favorite pastime—tractor tipping! Down the road a ways, Lightning McQueen and other citizens of Radiator Springs welcome you to Race Day and you'll cruise through either Luigi's Casa Della Tires or Ramone's House of Body Art. After that…it's time for the Main Event! As another car full of Guests pulls up next to you, Luigi and Guido start the race and off you go! You'll be neck and neck with the other car, diving and dipping up and down the open road at speeds of up to 40 MPH until you reach the black-and-white checkered finish line and find out which car is the winner!

HOT TIP

Smile! Your photo will be taken on this ride and you can buy a print near the exit.

SPY

Most **FastPass machines** are close to the attractions they go with but you'll find the ones for **Radiator Springs Racers** outside of Cars Land near **It's Tough to be a Bug.**

RATE THIS ATTRACTION

- ☐ Never. Again.
- ☐ Not so hot.
- ☐ Pretty cool…
- ☐ Way cool!
- ☐ Awesome!!
- ☐ AHH, MY FAVE!!!

One word I'd use to describe this attraction:

FUN FACT

When Radiator Springs Racers opened, it was the most expensive attraction ever built in any Disney theme park.

KA-CHOW!

HEY KIDS
COLOR
ME IN!

What color car did you ride in?

TIME MACHINE

2006
Six months after "Cars" hits theaters, concept art is released showing ideas for a new "Carland" in DCA.

2007
The Walt Disney Company announces DCA's major makeover, including Radiator Springs Racers as a major new attraction.

2009
Construction begins on Radiator Springs Racers, including the largest span of rockwork in any U.S. Disney park.

2012
Racers, start your engines! Radiator Springs Racers is an instant hit when it opens as part of Cars Land.

"I haven't gone this fast in years. I'm gonna blow a gasket or somethin'."
—SHERIFF

SHERIFF'S OLD

BiRTH of tHE BiLLBOARD

Along the path that runs beside **Radiator Springs Racers** you'll see a series of separate signs that, together, make a complete phrase. The **Burma-Shave** company installed rhyming signs like these in **1926** alongside a road in Minnesota. Motorists loved the funny eye-catching signs, the company's sales went up and the **billboard sign** was born.

MIND YOUR SPEED

AS YOU GO

SHERIFF'S OLD

BUT HE'S

NOT SLOW

FUN FACT
A geodesic dome, like you'll see at Fillmore's Taste-In, is made from connected, straight elements.

GROOVY!

★ Food & Drinks

Cozy Cone Motel

Don't let the name fool you—this isn't actually a motel but a cluster of traffic cone-shaped stands with outdoor tables. Each cone has a different menu and features a unique specialty drink—Doc's Wild Grape Tonic, Fillmore's Fuelin' Groovy All Natural Lemonade, Ramone's "Pear of Dice" Soda, Red's Apple Freeze and "Route" Beer Floats.

• *Churros* • *Filled bread cones* • *Flavored popcorn*
• *Pretzel bites* • *Soft-serve ice cream*

SPY Peek in the **window** of the Cozy Cone Motel office to find **Buzz Lightyear** hiding under a traffic cone, just like he does in *Toy Story 2.*

Fillmore's Taste-In

Named after the 1960s hippy-dippy van from the *Cars* movies, this colorful, tie-dyed dome has fresh, healthy snacks you can grab on the go.

• *Coconut water* • *Fruit* • *Tea* • *Veggies*

★ That's Entertainment

Cruising through Cars Land, DJ's Dance 'n' Drive is your chance to dance in the streets. Watch for a fancy blue car pulling over to party as carhop waitresses join in the fun and teach Guests how to shake it up.

Flo's V8 café

The perfect place to refuel, Flo named her vintage diner after a type of car engine. The retro decor will transport you back to simpler times as 1950s and 60s golden oldies play. Park it at a table out front or drive in to grab a booth at this quick-service pitstop.

• *Brioche French toast* • *Pie-o-rama*
• *Road gravel-topped milkshakes*
• *Rotisserie chicken*

SPY See if you can find a ginormous **car rear-view mirror** inside Flo's.

✳ MOTORAMA GIRLS MATCH-UP! ✳

Flo is a gleaming vintage showcar and **Motorama Girl**. Look for the image of **Flo** and the rest of this **all-girl singing group** on a wall inside **Flo's V8 Café** to figure out how to match these phrases with each car. The first one's been done for you. *Anwers on page 182.*

Flo → Sassy & Classy!

Laverne   She's Fin-Tastic!

Rhonda   Va-Va-Vroom!

Sheila   What a Creampuff!

113

★ Sample Souvenirs

LIGHTNING MCQUEEN LUNCHBOX

Over at Flo's V8 Café you can get a Kids' Meal OR you can pay a bit more for one served in a Lightning McQueen lunchbox to take home as a souvenir.

Usually Cast Members are **A-OK** with **kids at heart** ordering from the Kids' Menu too.

See how many words related to cars you can find on the **eye chart** inside Flo's V8 Café.

SUPER-CUTE SIPPERS

The Disneyland Resort sells many of their drinks in special Souvenir Sipper containers that you can take home as a souvenir. Two of the best can be found in Cars Land: retro milkshake glasses from Flo's V8 Café and oil cans from Cozy Cone Motel.

THE MAN BEHIND THE CARS

John Lasseter is a very busy guy. Not only is he the head of the creative department at Walt Disney Animation Studios and Pixar Animation Studios, he's also an advisor to the Disney Imagineers! John grew up 30 miles from **Disneyland** with his father who worked for the Chevrolet car company and his mother who was an art teacher. Growing up, he loved to draw and watch cartoons and in high school he read a book that changed his life, *Disney's Art of Animation* by Bob Thomas. Later, while in college studying animation, he got a summer job as a **Jungle Cruise skipper** in Disneyland! After graduating, John got his dream job as an **animator** for The Walt Disney Company and then moved on to LucasFilm where new ways to use **computers** for animation were being explored. LucasFilm branched off into **Pixar** and John eventually became the director of the world's first full-length computer-animated film, *Toy Story* in 1995. In 2000, John went on a family road trip along **Route 66** and got the idea for the movie *Cars*. When it came time to create Cars Land, he watched over every detail. When The Walt Disney Company bought Pixar in 2006, John was back working for Disney again. A true kid at heart, John collects vintage toys, model trains and **hawaiian shirts**—which he wears pretty much every day. John isn't a Disney Legend—**yet**—but he will be someday!

Toy Cars

If you have a favorite "car-acter" from *Cars*, you'll want to check out the cool toy vehicles at Sarge's Surplus Hut. Not only will you find the characters with their standard look, you'll also find *Star Wars* versions like Lightning McQueen as Luke Skywalker, Mater as Darth Vader and Ramone as Han Solo!

 SPY Don't miss the amazing light-up **model of Cars Land** located inside Sarge's Surplus Hut.

 ## Mini Quiz!

Can you guess what type of Jeep Sarge is?
Answer on page 182.
☐ Bantam Pilot   ☐ Ford GP   ☐ Willys MB

Bumper Sticker Bonanza!

Can you figure out which **bumper sticker** belongs to which **character**: Ariel, Belle, Captain Hook, Carl Fredricksen, Cruella de Vil, Fa Zhou, Grumpy, Nick Wilde or Woody. The first one's been done for you. *Answers on page 182.*

HONK IF YOU HAVE A SNAKE IN YER BOOT!

Woody

I brake for FORKS in the road!

If you can read this, you're too close.

I'D RATHER BE IN PARADISE FALLS

MY OTHER CAR IS A PIRATE SHIP

Proud Parent of a Daughter in the Imperial Army

PUPPIES On Board!

So many BOOKS, so little time!

SOME BUNNY LOVES ME

Beautiful neon lights brighten the night in Cars Land.

Pacific Wharf

What Will You Find in This Chapter?

ENTERTAINMENT
- Mariachi Divas

FOOD & DRINKS
- Alfresco Tasting Terrace
- Cocina Cucamonga Mexican Grill
- Ghirardelli Soda Fountain and Chocolate Shop
- Lucky Fortune Cookery
- Mendocino Terrace
- Pacific Wharf Café
- Sonoma Terrace
- Wine Country Trattoria

ACTIVITIES, GAMES & INFO
- ¡Buen Apetito!
- Fresh-Baked Fun
- The Sky's the Limit
- Disney Legend Close-Up: Burny Mattinson

MAP of PACIFIC WHARF

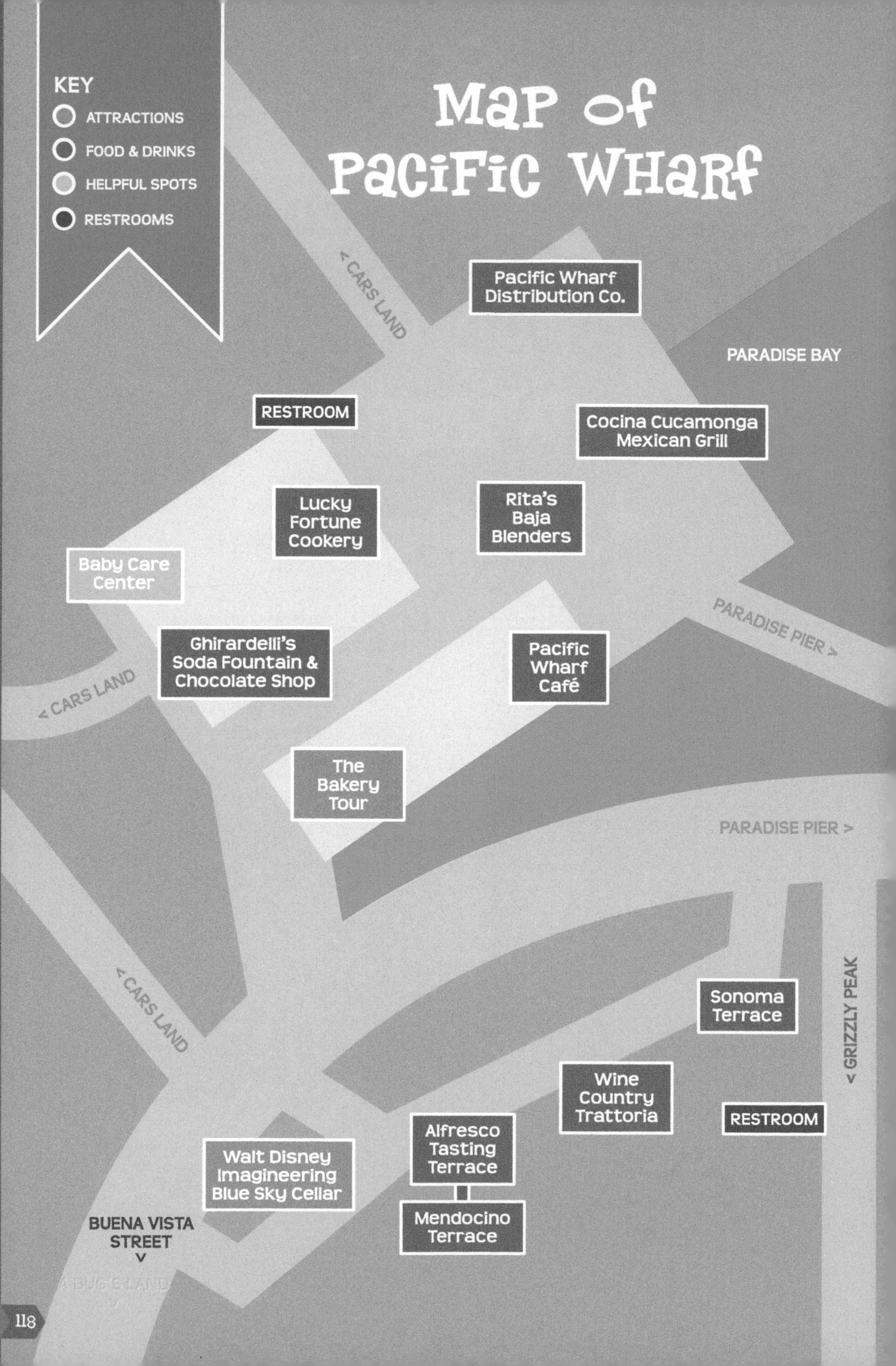

KEY
- ⚪ ATTRACTIONS
- ⚪ FOOD & DRINKS
- ⚪ HELPFUL SPOTS
- ⚫ RESTROOMS

< CARS LAND

PARADISE BAY

Pacific Wharf Distribution Co.

RESTROOM

Cocina Cucamonga Mexican Grill

Lucky Fortune Cookery

Rita's Baja Blenders

Baby Care Center

PARADISE PIER >

Ghirardelli's Soda Fountain & Chocolate Shop

Pacific Wharf Café

< CARS LAND

The Bakery Tour

PARADISE PIER >

< CARS LAND

Sonoma Terrace

< GRIZZLY PEAK

Wine Country Trattoria

RESTROOM

Walt Disney Imagineering Blue Sky Cellar

Alfresco Tasting Terrace

Mendocino Terrace

BUENA VISTA STREET
v

A BUG'S LAND

118

The Dock of the Bay

"Feed the birds and what have you got? Fat birds."
—MR. DAWES, SENIOR

Inspired by Northern California's Wine Country vineyards and the waterfront fishing and canning districts of San Francisco and Monterey, Pacific Wharf is the place to dock when you're ready to grab a bite. Because this land is made up almost entirely of eateries, it's sort of like the food court of Disney California Adventure. Choose from a variety of foods popular throughout California—from Mexican to Chinese to Italian and more. Enjoy a casual meal in the outdoor waterfront seating area near Paradise Bay or head over the bridge for fancier fare in the cluster of eateries across the way.

HOT TIP Be sure to check out the fishing net **photo spot** hanging over **Paradise Bay**. If the photo is taken from **the correct angle**, it will look like **YOU** are in the net of fish! See an **example** of this on page 5.

> NeVeR HaVe I eVeR Been to san FRancisco!

Waiting Game!

NEVER HAVE I EVER

All players starts with three fingers in the air. The first player says a true statement about themselves. For example, you could say "Never have I ever ridden on a *swinging* gondola on Mickey's Fun Wheel!" If any of the other people **have** done that, they must put down one finger. The next player makes their "Never have I ever..." statement and the game continues. The last person to have any fingers left in the air wins.

FUN FACT

The Ghirardelli Chocolate Company was founded in San Francisco in 1852 by Italian immigrant Domenico Ghirardelli.

GRAZIE!

★ # Food & Drinks

COCINA CUCAMONGA MEXICAN GRILL

Salsa on over to see what's cooking in this **cocina**—the Spanish word for kitchen. Named after a part of Los Angeles called Rancho Cucamonga, this grill serves up a variety of Mexican delights.

• *Beef burrito* • *Chicken caesar salad* • *Fire-grilled chicken*

GHIRARDELLI SODA FOUNTAIN AND CHOCOLATE SHOP

Part ice cream parlor and part shop, this is the place to satisfy your sweet tooth —or pick up a packaged treat to give as a gift. Right outside the entrance are several tables where you can relax and enjoy your goodies.

• *Banana split* • *Hot chocolate* • *Hot fudge sundae*

 HOT TIP When you walk in a Ghirardelli shop you are given a **free chocolate sample.** Their shop in DCA is no different, so pop in if you're a chocolate fan.

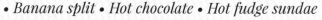

¡BUEN APETITO! (ENJOY YOUR MEAL)

Not sure what some of the items are on the menu at **Cocina Cucamonga Mexican Grill**? Here's the rundown. Which ones sound **"delicioso"** to you?

※ **Burrito Sonora**
Flour tortilla folded in a cylinder shape with beef or chicken, cheese, onions and peppers

※ **Carne Asada**
Marinated steak cooked with a charred or lightly burnt flavor

※ **Chicken Tamales**
Steamed cornmeal filled with shredded chicken

※ **Fajita Salad**
Grilled strips of meat mixed with beans, lettuce, onions and peppers

※ **Quesadilla**
A round flour tortilla folded in half with melted cheese inside

※ **Tacos Monterrey**
Soft flour tortillas folded in half with beef or chicken, peppers, onion and cheese inside

Lucky Fortune Cookery

Do you like to customize your meals? Then this is your lucky day! This quick-service spot with colorful paper lanterns serves rice bowls where you mix n' match the topping of your choice with the sauce of your choice to create your meal just the way you like it. The best part is that every order comes with a fortune cookie for dessert.
• *Asian rice bowl* • *Edamame* • *Mango slices*

Pacific Wharf café

Inspired by the cafés of Fisherman's Wharf in San Francisco, the specialty here is soup served in a freshly made bread bowl from The Bakery Tour next door.
• *Hot cocoa* • *Soup in a bread bowl*
• *Turkey sandwich*

 ## That's Entertainment

Olé! An all-female, Grammy-winning mariachi band, **The Mariachi Divas**, perform in Pacific Wharf and on Paradise Pier's Paradise Garden Bandstand.

Fresh-Baked Fun

Pacific Wharf is home to **The Bakery Tour**—a self-guided, walk-through experience where you'll learn how Boudin sourdough bread is made. Isidore Boudin, the son of a family of master bakers in France, went to America during the California Gold Rush in 1849.
He didn't find gold but struck it rich when he blended the goldminers' sourdough with French breadmaking techniques.

 HOT TIP The Bakery Tour gives out **free bread samples** when you enter. Combine that with your **free chocolate sample** from Ghirardelli's Soda Fountain and Chocolate Shop to make an awesome sandwich!

THe SKY'S tHe Limit

From time to time, **Walt Disney Imagineering Blue Sky Cellar** shows exhibits about features coming to the Disneyland Resort. Guests can see concept art by Imagineers and watch short films that explain the creative process from the brainstorming phase where "the sky's the limit" to the finished product. Exhibits have included:

- Fantasy Faire
- Market House
- Mickey's Fun Wheel
- World of Color

This area is sometimes used for special events.

Was this open when you visited?
■ Yes ■ No
If yes, what was it like?

- - - - - - - - - - - - - - - - -

- - - - - - - - - - - - - - - - -

- - - - - - - - - - - - - - - - -

aLfResco TasTing TeRRace

To dine *alfresco* is to eat outdoors in the fresh air. You'll find a few snacks here but the main event at this lounge is the wine flights where grown-ups can sample tastes of several different wines. For the younger set, there's a kids' punch with a light-up character clipped on the side.
- *Ariel or Lightning McQueen punch*
- *Beef sliders* • *Salad* • *Shrimp*

MenDocino TeRRace

Similar to Alfresco Tasting Terrace, this is an outdoor lounge with a few snacks and a large selection of wine for grown-ups. The name comes from the beautiful coastal town of Mendocino in Northern California.
- *Cold meat & cheese box*
- *Non-alcoholic sparkling cider*

Sonoma TeRRace

This outdoor quick-service terrace specializes in craft beers from California. Sonoma Valley in Northern California is famous for winemaking but it also has breweries (where beer is made), distilleries (where hard alcohol is made) and cideries (where cider is made).
- *Gourmet cheese plate*
- *Non-alcoholic sparkling cider* • *Pretzels*

Hidden Mickey?!

Wine Country Trattoria

The vine-covered walls and tile floors and roofs create a European countryside atmosphere at this charming **trattoria**—a type of casual Italian café. One of the special features here is "Pasta Your Way" where you can choose which type of pasta you want and what you'd like on it. With a full menu of appetizers, salads, main dishes, desserts and specialty coffee drinks, this is definitely a spot where you can sit and stay awhile.

• Ariel or Lightning McQueen punch • Pizza • Salad • Tiramisù

Mini Quiz!

Can you guess what the name is for this type of architecture found in the city of San Francisco?
Answer on page 182.

☐ Craftsman
☐ Tudor
☐ Victorian

Disney Legend Close-Up: Burny Mattinson

Burny Mattinson was born in San Francisco and was amazed by the movie *Pinocchio* at the Orpheum Theatre when he was a little boy. Growing up, Burny loved to draw and watch cartoons and when he found out people could actually do animation as a **career** he knew what he wanted to do. Later, his family moved to Los Angeles and, when he graduated from high school, his mother drove him to the entrance of the **Walt Disney Studios** with a portfolio of his artwork. The guard at the gate looked at the drawings and helped Burny to get a job in the mailroom. Even though Burny had **no formal art training**, he worked his way up in the company and made it into the animation department where he worked on **animated classics** like *Lady and the Tramp*, *The Sword in the Stone*, *Robin Hood*, *The Lion King* and many more. Recently, he worked as a **storyboard artist** on *Zootopia*. Burny was named a Disney Legend in 2008.

You'll feel like you're visiting the city by the bay when you stop off for a bite in Pacific Wharf.

PARADISE PIER

What Will You Find in This Chapter?

ATTRACTIONS
- California Screamin'
- Golden Zephyr
- Goofy's Sky School
- Jumpin' Jellyfish
- King Triton's Carousel
- Mickey's Fun Wheel
- Silly Symphony Swings
- The Little Mermaid ~ Ariel's Undersea Adventure
- Toy Story Midway Mania

ENTERTAINMENT
- Operation: Playtime
- Paradise Garden Bandstand
- World of Color

FOOD & DRINKS
- Ariel's Grotto
- Boardwalk Pizza & Pasta
- Corn Dog Castle
- Cove Bar
- Don Tomas
- Hot Dog Hut
- Paradise Garden Grill
- Paradise Pier Ice Cream Co.

MEET N' GREETS
- Buzz Lightyear
- Jessie
- Woody

SHOPS
- Boardwalk Bazaar
- Embarcadero Gifts
- Midway Mercantile
- Point Mugu Tattoo
- Seaside Souvenirs
- Sideshow Shirts
- Treasures in Paradise

ACTIVITIES, GAMES & INFO
- Spin n' Point!
- See You in the Funny Papers!
- Goofy Fun!
- It's All Greek to Me
- Sample Souvenirs
- Hurry, Hurry, Hurry, Step Right Up!
- Super Sidekicks!

MAP of PARADISE PIER

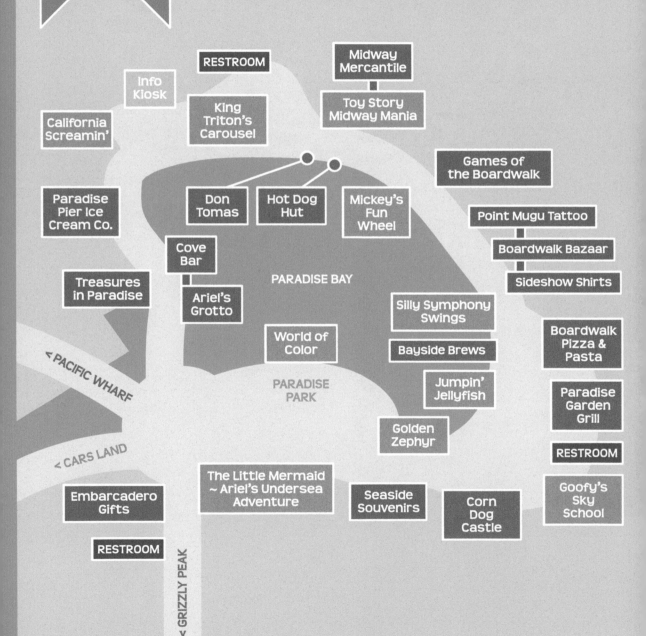

KEY
- ATTRACTIONS
- FOOD & DRINKS
- HELPFUL SPOTS
- RESTROOMS
- SHOPS

RESTROOM

Info Kiosk

Midway Mercantile

California Screamin'

King Triton's Carousel

Toy Story Midway Mania

Games of the Boardwalk

Paradise Pier Ice Cream Co.

Don Tomas

Hot Dog Hut

Mickey's Fun Wheel

Point Mugu Tattoo

Boardwalk Bazaar

Cove Bar

Sideshow Shirts

Treasures in Paradise

PARADISE BAY

Ariel's Grotto

World of Color

Silly Symphony Swings

Boardwalk Pizza & Pasta

< PACIFIC WHARF

Bayside Brews

PARADISE PARK

Jumpin' Jellyfish

Paradise Garden Grill

< CARS LAND

Golden Zephyr

RESTROOM

The Little Mermaid ~ Ariel's Undersea Adventure

Seaside Souvenirs

Goofy's Sky School

Embarcadero Gifts

Corn Dog Castle

RESTROOM

< GRIZZLY PEAK

A Slice of Paradise

Festooned with striped awnings, latticed woodwork and twinkling lights, Paradise Pier is a celebration of the seaside amusement parks of yesteryear. Paradise Pier doesn't go out over the water like a traditional **pier** but instead wraps around a large lake called Paradise Bay. Stroll the wooden boardwalk past vintage-style billboards to take your pick from the many attractions. This hotspot for fun has more rides than any other land!

> SO YOU KNOW...
> pier = structure built on posts that goes out over water

Hmm Hmm Hmm Hmm, Hmm-Hmm Hmm Hmm-Hmm Hmm Hmm...

Waiting Game!

HUM THAT TUNE

Hum the tune to a Disney song and see if the other people in your group can guess what song it is. If no one can guess it, try giving the other players a hint by acting out the words of the song. If the other players *still* can't guess the song, hum and then sing a word when you come to the place in the song where that word would be.

MAY BE SCARY

★ California Screamin'

ROLLER COASTER * —est.— 2001 * WILD & THRILLING

Are you ready, Screamers? The fun begins when the coaster coasts its way to the launch zone alongside Paradise Bay. What happens next is sort of like being shot out of a cannon so be sure you're looking straight ahead with your head back against the seat! After a countdown from 5, you'll rocket forward reaching the ride's top speed of 55 miles per hour in about four seconds, looping completely upside down around a giant sun and dipping up and down hills like a wave in the ocean!

FUN FACT

California Screamin' looks like an old-fashioned wooden roller coaster but it's actually built out of steel— 5,800,000 pounds of steel.

AWESOME!

HOT TIP — **Cheese!** Your photo will be taken mid-scream during this ride and can be purchased near the exit at the **California Scream Cam** stand.

SPY — Sitting this ride out? Be sure to find a spot **near the water** to watch the ride cars speed out of the **launch zone.**

California SCREAMIN'

🎀 Mini Quiz!

Wooden roller coasters became popular in the late 1800s at seaside amusement parks but can you guess which of these was the world's first **tubular steel** roller coaster?

Answer on page 182.

- ☐ Disneyland's Matterhorn Bobsleds
- ☐ Magic Kingdom's Space Mountain
- ☐ Tokyo DisneySea's Raging Spirits

Photograph by Dave DeCaro • http://davelandweb.com

TIME MACHINE

1965
The Mamas & the Papas release their mega-popular version of the song "California Dreamin'."

2001
DCA opens with California Screamin' as its largest, most thrilling attraction. Totally tubular!

2010
Actor Neil Patrick Harris becomes the new voice of California Screamin'. "Not ready? Too bad!"

2012
California Screamin' earns the title of World's Longest Looping Roller Coaster.

Fun Facts about California Screamin'

The blue tubes you ride through are "scream tubes" which bounce the rider's shouts back into the park so the sounds don't disturb the neighbors.

This is the fastest ride in the Disneyland Resort.

The track is 6,072 feet long with a 108-foot drop, 120 feet off the ground.

In 2007, the ride temporarily changed to Rockin' California Screamin' & featured the song "Around the World" by the Red Hot Chili Peppers.

When it was built, this was the third-longest roller coaster in the U.S. & the eighth-longest in the world. Then, in 2006, it became the longest *looping* roller coaster in the entire world.

Riders have not always looped around the sun. What is now Mickey's Fun Wheel used to have a sun & this ride had a Mickey Mouse head.

FUN FACT

Long ago, knights improved their horse-riding skills by galloping in a circle & tossing balls to each other. By the 18th century, carousels that recreated this game were hugely popular at fairs all around Europe.

WHOA!

"As long as you live under my ocean, you'll obey my rules!"
—KING TRITON

★ King Triton's Carousel

MERRY-GO-ROUND
— EST —
2001
CALM & MELLOW

Hold on tight and enjoy your *swim!* Inspired by *The Little Mermaid,* Ariel's father King Triton is the *host* with the *most* of this classic ride with a twist. While carousels usually have *horses,* King Triton has saddled up *sea creatures* instead—seven species found in the waters off California's Coast. Hop on the *bejeweled* underwater friend of your choice or a water chariot and enjoy a *gentle cruise* under the sea.

SPY Take a look at the top of the carousel to see **swirly frames** with picture-perfect scenes from California's most famous **oceanside piers and parks.**

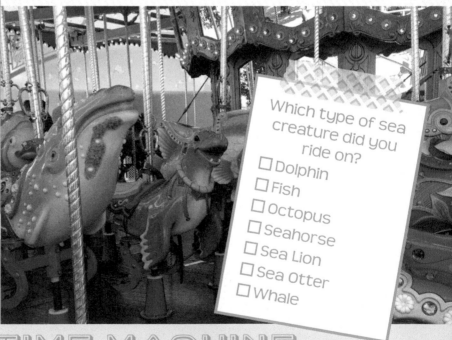

Which type of sea creature did you ride on?
- ☐ Dolphin
- ☐ Fish
- ☐ Octopus
- ☐ Seahorse
- ☐ Sea Lion
- ☐ Sea Otter
- ☐ Whale

TIME MACHINE

900 B.C.	1837	1989	2001
In Greek mythology, Triton is the messenger of the sea. He carries a trident & blows a conch shell to change the waves.	*"The Little Mermaid" by Hans Christian Andersen is first published. In the story, the mermaid & her father are not named.*	*King Triton is Ariel's father when Disney's version of "The Little Mermaid" hits theaters.*	*Splash! King Triton's Carousel is an Opening Day attraction in DCA.*

KING Triton's Carousel

SPY

See if you can find an
octopus holding a flag
on King Triton's Carousel.

HEY KIDS
COLOR
ME IN!

FUN FACT

When working on "Toy Story," animators at Pixar attached boards to their shoes & walked around so they could understand how the Green Army Men moved.

WOW!

> "I can't stop Andy from growing up... but I wouldn't miss it for the world."
> —WOODY

Toy Story Midway Mania

SHOOTING GALLERY RIDE · —EST.— **2008** · LIVELY & EXCITING

Grab your 3D glasses, hop on a two-sided ride car and shrink to the size of a toy as you spin through a colorful playland of carnival games in Andy's Room. Take aim at various targets and pull the string on your Spring-Action Shooter to see how many points you can score. But, don't worry, you'll get to practice first and the Toy Story gang will show you just what to do—and then cheer you on along the way. You'll zip past alphabet blocks, board games, crayons and more as you move from game to game. At the end you'll find out how many points you earned, who got the highest score in your ride car and which virtual animal is your prize.

 HOT TIP

Want to score **big**? Take time to aim for targets with **higher point values.** At the end when the mine carts are coming at you, fire at them as **quickly** as possible—the faster you hit the bullseyes, the more they'll be worth!

 SPY

As you exit this attraction, notice the **Toy Story Midway Games Play Set** (like the one you just rode through) on the floor.

Photograph by Dave DeCaro • http://davelandweb.com

TIME MACHINE

1995
"Toy Story" hits theaters & is the first of many movies starring Woody & Buzz.

2006
Pacific Coast Photos & Malibu-Ritos close to make way for a "Toy Story" attraction.

2008
Toy Story Midway Mania opens in Disney California Adventure. "Oooooooooooooooo!"

2010
The ride's dart-throwing game changes from Bo Peep's Baaa-loon Pop to Rex & Trixie's Dino Darts.

Spin n' Point!

In this game for two or more players, close your eyes and, as another person spins this book, point and put your finger down on this page. Do the activity that's closest to where your finger lands. Some activities are for one player, others are for all players. Whichever player gets **20 points** or more first wins the game.

See who can stand on one foot the longest. First to lose loses **1 point**.
(If this takes awhile, continue playing)

Find something around you that there is only one of & win **5 points**.
(If this space is landed on more than once, players must find a new item each time)

Andy's coming —EVERYONE FREEZE! Last player to move wins **5 points**.

Don't make a peep! If you talk before the next player takes their turn you lose **1 point**.

Think of a *Toy Story* character. The player who guesses who you are wins **1 point**.
(Players guess in order of age, youngest goes first)

Close your eyes & have another player spin you. Guess which way you're facing when you stop & win **5 points**.

Find something around you that's red & win **5 points**.
(If this space is landed on more than once, players must find a new item each time)

Sid ties you to a rocket. You lose **1 point**.

★ Meet n' Greets

Stop and play with Buzz Lightyear, Jessie or Woody across from Mickey's Fun Wheel!

133

FUN FACT

An eccentric wheel is different from a Ferris wheel because some of the gondolas slide on rails as the wheel rotates.

AH!

"And he'll sweep me off my feet. And I'll know he's the one when he makes me laugh."
—MINNIE MOUSE

MAY BE SCARY ⚠

★ Mickey's Fun Wheel

ECCENTRIC WHEEL
EST. 2001
LIVELY & EXCITING

You can't miss Mickey's Fun Wheel! This 160-foot tall ride looms large over Paradise Pier with Mickey Mouse's smiling face in the center. Choose a mellow stationary gondola that moves along with the entire wheel or a wild swinging gondola that careens across an oval track. As you ride, enjoy grand views of the Disneyland Resort.

 HOT TIP Be sure to get in the **correct line** for the type of gondola you want. There's a reason the swinging gondolas have **barf bags!**

Minnie Bow Patch by Aaron Albarran • www.manandthemouse.com | Illustration by Gabrielle Jean • www.littlemoondance.storenvy.com

TIME MACHINE

1928
The world says "Hiya pal!" to Mickey Mouse when his "Steamboat Willie" cartoon becomes a hit.

2001
Sun Wheel is an Opening Day attraction in DCA.

2009
Sun Wheel is rethemed & reopens as Mickey's Fun Wheel. Yippee!

2013
The Fun Wheel Challenge launches where Guests play to win control of the lights on Mickey's Fun Wheel.

See you in the Funny Papers!

Mickey Mouse is a popular guy! After the short cartoon *Steamboat Willie* made him a star, **Mickey Mouse Clubs** sprung up all over the country. At the start of 1930, the Mickey Mouse **comic strip** debuted, at first written by **Walt Disney** and drawn by **Ub Iwerks.** Soon, new comic strips followed featuring characters like Bambi, Bucky Bug, Donald Duck, José Carioca and Pluto.

Ready to star in your own comic? Draw a **three-panel comic strip** in each of the three rows below about your adventures in DCA. Write the **title** above each strip and sign the bottom right corner of the last panel.

TITLE: _____

TITLE: _____

TITLE: _____

FUN FACT

The "William Tell Overture" is part of an opera based on Swiss hero William Tell, written in the 1800s by Gioachino Rossini. The legend goes that William Tell was such an expert with a bow & arrow that he shot an apple off his son's head.....

YIKES!

★ Silly Symphony Swings

Wave Swinger
★ —est.— ★
2001
Lively & exciting

There's one perfect word to capture how you'll feel on this ride: Whee! First, you'll take a seat on a single or double swing. As the dramatic notes of the William Tell Overture play, the red-and-white canopy that holds the swings lifts and rotates around the center column. Once the ride picks up speed, the canopy will gently tilt one way and then another as you soar through the sky over Paradise Bay.

HOT TIP

Riders between **40"–48" tall** can only ride on a double swing and must be accompanied by someone **over 48" tall.** There are different lines for the different types of swings.

SPY

Look at the very tip top of this ride to see **Mickey Mouse** in a conductor's uniform holding a baton.

Photograph by Dave DeCaro • http://davelandweb.com

TIME MACHINE

1929	1935	2001	2010
The Walt Disney Company begins releasing Silly Symphonies—short cartoons with the action set to music.	In the Silly Symphony cartoon "The Band Concert," Mickey & his band play the William Tell Overture during a storm.	Orange Stinger is an Opening Day attraction in DCA.	Orange Stinger is rethemed & reopens as Silly Symphony Swings. Bravo!

136

★ Goofy's Sky School

Learn to fly the Goofy way! Climb aboard an airplane that says *Student Pilot* on the back, and take off on a dipping-and-diving jaunt. Just when you go *one way*, you'll go *another* as the track zigs and zags past a series of signs that lay out the lesson plan. You'll graduate from this school with *flying* colors!

Wild Mouse Coaster ★ est. 2001 ★ Lively & exciting

SPY
Goofy made his Sky School from a **chicken farm**. While you're in line, see if you can find the **parachutes** made from **chicken-feed bags**.

FUN FACT

Wild Mouse coasters don't have big hills & loops like some other roller coasters. Instead, they take quick, tight turns that make you feel like your ride car is about to fly off the tracks. They turn so quickly that riders can feel the g-forces pulling against them.

GAWRSH!!

"We should slow down before we break the sound barrier!"
—GOOFY

Goofy Fun!

Fill in the missing letters from the lesson signs at Goofy's Sky School. The first one's been done for you.
Answers on page 182.

LESSON 1
How to T A K E O F F

LESSON 2
How to F _ Y

LESSON 3
How to T _ R _

LESSON 4
How to N _ _ S _ D _ V _ _

LESSON 5
How to L _ N _

TIME MACHINE

1932
Goofy makes his debut in the short cartoon "Mickey's Revue." Gee willikers!

1940
The short cartoon "Goofy's Glider" is one of Goofy's famous "How To" cartoons & later inspires Goofy's Sky School.

2001
Mulholland Madness, based on the winding Mulholland Drive in Los Angeles, is an Opening Day attraction in DCA.

2011
Mulholland Madness is rethemed & reopens as Goofy's Sky School.

FUN FACT
A group of jellyfish is called a smack or a fluther.

HA!

★ Jumpin' Jellyfish

OUTDOOR DROP TOWER
— EST. —
2001
Lively & exciting

Jump for joy as you float up and down on a *jellyfish* built for two. Two tall towers decorated with seaweed, fish and starfish from *under the sea* sit side by side and hold six jellyfish each.

Take a seat, sit back and enjoy as your jellyfish lifts you 40-feet into the air and *gracefully glides* to the ground and back up again.

HOT TIP Jumpin' Jellyfish—and other Paradise Pier attractions—**don't jump** during **World of Color.** See the complete list on page 43.

SPY Try to find a **speaker** shaped like a **sand dollar** near Jumpin' Jellyfish. Check out the photo on **page 5** to see what you're looking for.

Illustration by Michalina Grzegorz • www.etsy.com/shop/sketchesofmichelle

★ Golden Zephyr

Orbit the skies of the Golden State of California in a sleek, silver spaceship! Decked out with retro fins and shining chrome, the ride cars hang from a central tower lined in twinkling lights. With six rows of seats per ride car, this is a ride larger groups can enjoy together.

SO YOU KNOW...
zephyr = gentle breeze

Rotating Spaceships
— est —
2001
Lively & Exciting

HOT TIP This ride may be named after a **breeze** but it does **not** not run in windy weather!

HEY KIDS
COLOR
ME IN!

FUN FACT
The vintage look of Golden Zephyr is inspired by 1920s & 30s science-fiction stories such as Buck Rogers & Flash Gordon.

ROGER!

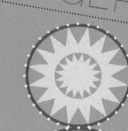

★ That's Entertainment

Atten-tion! The Green Army Men from the *Toy Story* movies pile in their Jeep and pull over throughout Paradise Pier and display their awesome drumming skills for **Operation: Playtime!** The soldiers are searching for recruits and are ready to train YOU!

FUN FACT

The large dome at the entrance to the Little Mermaid ride is inspired by San Francisco's Palace of Fine Arts. This building was part of the 1915 Panama–Pacific Exposition & still stands today.

ROAD TRIP!

★ The Little Mermaid ~ Ariel's Undersea Adventure

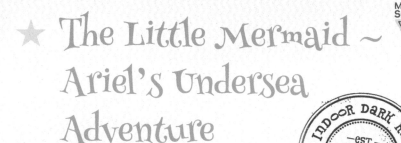

INDOOR DARK RIDE
— est. —
2011
CALM & MELLOW

Climb into a colorful clamshell and dive into the tale of Ariel the Little Mermaid. After Scuttle the Seagull sees you on your way, you'll coast through Ariel's underwater world to find her singing among the treasures she's found in the human world. From there it's on to a festive dance party with Sebastian the Crab and his ocean friends. Things take a dark turn when you pass the moray eels Flotsam and Jetsam and their master Ursula the Sea Witch who is crooning about her collection of poor unfortunate souls. Next, Ariel and Prince Eric share a romantic rowboat ride in an enchanting lagoon. When the two lovebirds kiss at last, Ursula's evil spell is broken and it's time for a wedding—and time to wave farewell to the Prince and Princess as they live happily ever after.

SPY Near the end of your adventure, keep an eye out for a **small cabinet** with an oval cameo on each door. The image on the left is of **Hans Christian Andersen** and the one on the right is of **The Little Mermaid** —a famous statue in Denmark where Hans Christian Andersen was from.

TIME MACHINE

1837
"The Little Mermaid" by author Hans Christian Andersen is first published.

1989
Life is the bubbles! "The Little Mermaid" hits theaters.

2001
"Golden Dreams," a movie about Californian history, is an Opening Day attraction in DCA.

2011
Three years after "Golden Dreams" closes, The Little Mermaid ~ Ariel's Undersea Adventure opens in the same spot.

"If you want to cross the bridge, my sweet,
you've got to pay the toll."
—URSULA

141

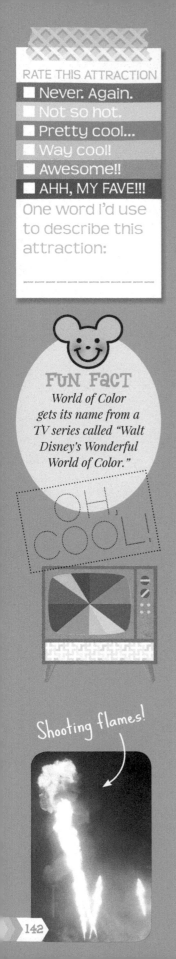

FUN FACT

World of Color gets its name from a TV series called "Walt Disney's Wonderful World of Color."

OH, COOL!

Shooting flames!

"The world we live in would look pretty dull if Mother Nature used a black-and-white palette."
—WALT DISNEY

Dancing fountains!

★ World of Color

Water Show Spectacular • Lively & Exciting • est. 2010

$\mathcal{F}$ind a spot along the shores of Paradise Bay to catch this dramatic spectacular that takes a look back at famous moments in The Walt Disney Company's rich history. Though World of Color changes its theme from time to time, the format of the show is the same. Clips are shown on enormous screens made of water mist and on Mickey's Fun Wheel. In front of the projections, special effects—including carpets of fog, colorful dancing fountains, lasers and shooting flames—make the waters of Paradise Bay come alive with action and drama.

HOT TIP
To enter the World of Color viewing areas at Paradise Park, you must have a **FastPass**—which is available near Grizzly River Run. If you don't have one, you can watch the show from various spots around **Paradise Pier**.

★ Food & Drinks

SO YOU KNOW...
grotto =
watery cavern

ARIEL'S GROTTO

Walk under a giant seashell and down a spiral staircase to enjoy breakfast and lunchtime Character Dining where Ariel and her princess pals will meet n' greet with you. The **grotto** also serves dinner but by that time the princesses have swum away for the day.

• *Fresh catch of the day* • *Pasta* • *Scrambled eggs*

Woo hoo! Kids and kids at heart can get a **paper crown** with stickers and other goodies during their meal at Ariel's Grotto.

DID YOU EAT IN PARADISE PIER?
☐ Yes   ☐ No
If yes, where?

_____

What'd ya have?

_____

_____

Was it good?
☐ Yes   ☐ No
☐ Maybe So

FUN FACT
Cove Bar is SO popular that a gazebo was recently removed to expand the seating area. The expansion was a great idea but it's STILL tough to score a table.

DANG!

COVE BAR

When you're ready to take a break, this full-service, outdoor spot upstairs from Ariel's Grotto has some of the best views in town. There are hearty snacks and fancy specialty cocktails as well as fun drinks for kids like cotton candy lemonade with a puff of cotton candy on the straw.

• *Buffalo wings* • *Lobster nachos* • *Pizza*

If **World of Color** is starting soon, hang out at **Cove Bar** for a **pretty good**—though **kinda sideways**—view of the show.

143

Boardwalk Pizza & Pasta

Will you visit the Pizza Station, the Pasta Station or the Salad Station? Take your pick at this quick-service restaurant and then find a table in the large outdoor seating area nearby.

• *Meatball sandwich* • *Pasta* • *Pizza* • *Salad*

 Look **inside** Boardwalk Pizza & Pasta to spy a **Pinocchio** toy sitting on a shelf.

Corn Dog Castle

Corn dogs reign supreme at this on-the-go stand with nearby seating. Choose which type of corn dog you'd like (spicy or regular) and whether you'd like sliced apples or chips to go with it.

• *Cheddar cheese stick* • *Corn dog*

Don Tomas

Channel your inner caveman with a jumbo turkey leg from this on-the-go stand that serves "The Midway's Best Bites." **Don** is a Spanish title for someone of distinction so, in English, the name of this stand would be Sir Thomas.

• *Chimichanga* • *Corn on the cob* • *Turkey leg*

Hot Dog Hut

Grab a dog and go at this red-and-white striped spot right next to Mickey's Fun Wheel.

• *Chips* • *Corn on the cob* • *Hot dog*

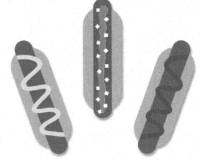

 When you're near Hot Dog Hut, look around to see if you can find the **Donald Duck trim** pictured at the bottom of this page!

★ That's Entertainment

Check out the **Paradise Garden Bandstand** in front of Boardwalk Pizza & Pasta to enjoy various types of live music like Irish Celtic, Jazz & Mariachi.

PARADISE PIER ICE CREAM CO.

Look for the cheerful, striped awning and you've found this hotspot for on-the-go cool treats.
- *Beachfront float*
- *Soft-serve ice cream*

PARADISE GARDEN GRILL

This on-the-go stand serves up **Mediterranean** skewers with your choice of sauce. There's even a dessert skewer with brownies, strawberries and chocolate syrup!
- *Baklava*
- *Greek salad*
- *Skewers*

> SO YOU KNOW...
> **Mediterranean** = countries on the border of the Mediterranean Sea

Snack carts are dotted all around DCA!

IT'S ALL GREEK TO ME

Not sure what some of the **exotic items** are on the menu at **Paradise Garden Grill**? Here's the rundown on some of the things you can choose from. Which one sounds like **paradise** to you?

Baklava
Dessert made from thin layers of pastry soaked in sweet syrup and filled with chopped walnuts

Chimichurri
Spicy meat sauce made with chili pepper flakes, garlic, olive oil, parsley and vinegar

Feta
White, salty cheese made from goat's milk

Pepperoncini
Hot chili pepper

Pita Bread
Flat, hollow bread that can be split open to hold a filling—sometimes called pocket bread

Rice Pilaf
Rice cooked in a broth with fruit, nuts or vegetables

Tofu
Bean curd made from edamame (soy beans)

Tzatziki
Sauce made from cucumbers, garlic and plain Greek yogurt

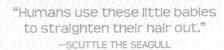

"Humans use these little babies to straighten their hair out."
—SCUTTLE THE SEAGULL

★ Sample Souvenirs

Cute Caricature

A **caricature** is a drawing where certain parts of the subject's face are made bigger or more exaggerated than they are in real life. You can sit for your very own caricature portrait across from the entrance to Ariel's Grotto.

 There are also caricature artists in **New Orleans Square** in Disneyland.

Darling Dinglehopper

In *The Little Mermaid,* Ariel finds a fork from the human world and has no idea what it's called or how to use it. Scuttle the Seagull, who likes to pretend he knows what he's talking about, tells Ariel that humans use dinglehoppers to style their hair! You can get your very own dinglehopper hairbrush at Embarcadero Gifts.

Long-Lasting Balloon

If you're put off by the price of the balloons, the good news is that they last a long, *long* time and, if your balloon accidentally pops while you're in the park, it can be replaced for free!

 Just ask and the **Cast Members** who walk around selling balloons will usually let you hold the **entire bunch** for an awesome photo!

Illustration by Aaron Albarran • www.manandthemouse.com

Hurry, Hurry, Hurry, Step Right Up!

The main walkway through the **1893 Chicago World's Fair** was lined with various shows and games and was called the **Midway Plaisance**. Because of this, fairs and carnivals call their main walkways **"midways."** Traveling entertainers had offered customers carnival-style games before but this fair was the start of their popularity in America. In DCA, you can play carnival games for prizes (for an extra fee) at **Games of the Boardwalk.**

All of these things were at the Chicago World's Fair in 1893—except for one. Can you put a ✔ in the box next to the fake? *Answer on page 182.*

☐ Cotton candy

☐ Hula dancers

☐ Pressed coins

☐ Replica of a Viking ship

☐ Travelator (moving walkway)

☐ World's first Ferris wheel

SUPER SIDEKICKS!

From Ariel to Zeus, every Disney hero seems to have a sidekick. Draw a trail of bubbles (or a line) to match the **hero** with their **sidekick**. The first one's been done for you. *Answers on page 182.*

FLit

BaLoo

FLOUNDER

TiNKeR BeLL

Ariel

Bambi

Kristoff

Mickey Mouse

THuMPeR

Mowgli

Mulan

Peter Pan

SVen

Pocahontas

HeRMeS

Rapunzel

Zeus

PLuto

MuSHu

PascaL

Learn to fly in five easy lessons at Goofy's Sky School.

GOOFY'S SKY SCHOOL

FLY THE GOOFY WAY!

GRiZZLy PeaK

What Will You Find in This Chapter?

MAP of GRIZZLY PEAK

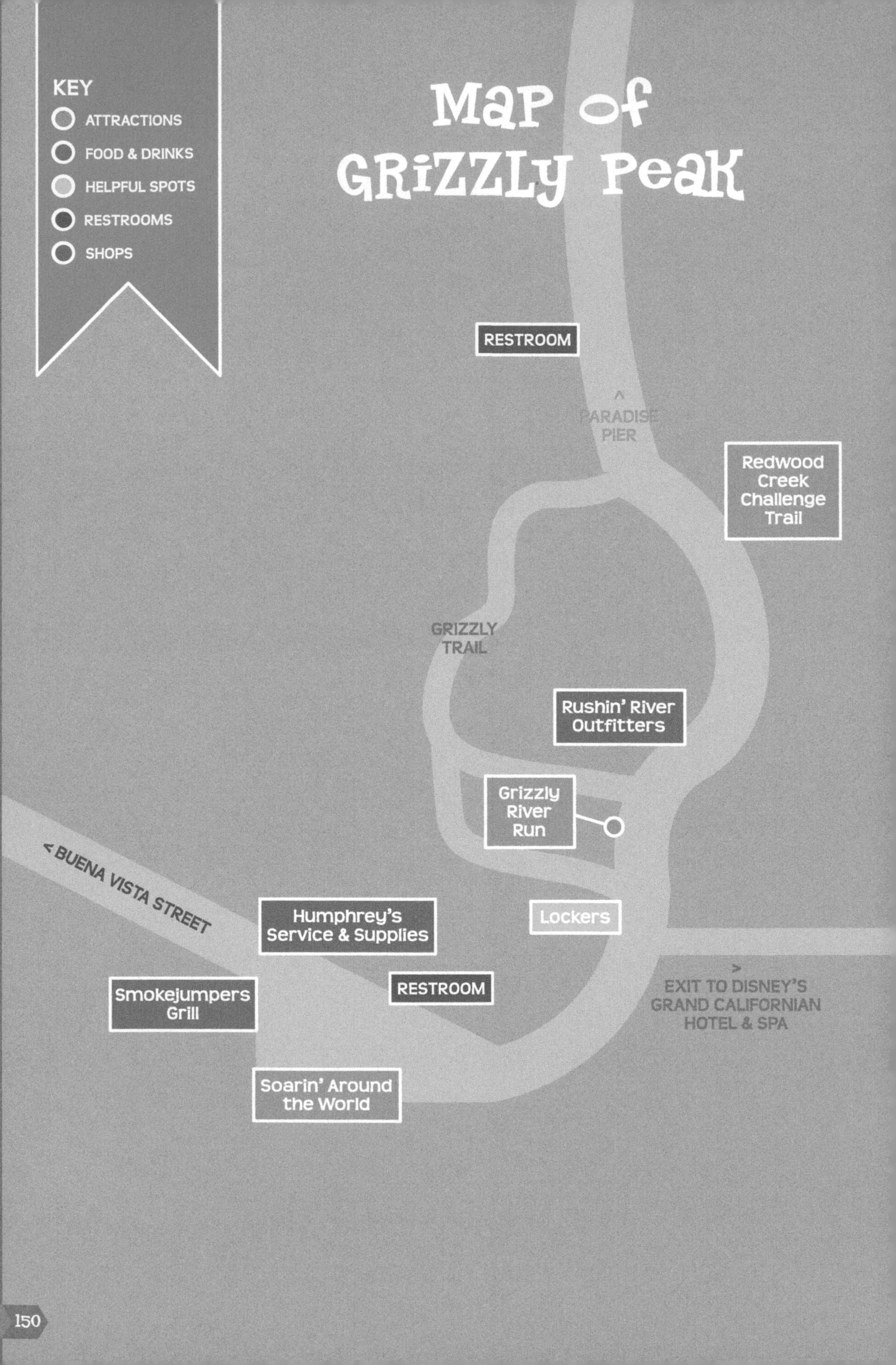

KEY
- ○ ATTRACTIONS
- ○ FOOD & DRINKS
- ◑ HELPFUL SPOTS
- ● RESTROOMS
- ○ SHOPS

RESTROOM

∧
PARADISE
PIER

Redwood
Creek
Challenge
Trail

GRIZZLY
TRAIL

Rushin' River
Outfitters

Grizzly
River
Run

◀ BUENA VISTA STREET

Lockers

Humphrey's
Service & Supplies

RESTROOM

>
EXIT TO DISNEY'S
GRAND CALIFORNIAN
HOTEL & SPA

Smokejumpers
Grill

Soarin' Around
the World

Fun at Its Peak

Travel back in time to enjoy the vintage charm of California's scenic national parks in the 1950s and 60s. Grizzly Peak is named after the roaring bear-shaped mountain that rises above the pine trees, a famous symbol of Disney California Adventure. The winding lanes of this rustic retreat are flanked by trees, plants and flowers native to the West Coast. This land is also home to Grizzly Peak Airfield, a tribute to firefighters who battle wildfires in forests and national parks.

 SPY Peek into the **vintage station wagon** near Humphrey's Service & Supplies and you'll see it's loaded up for a family camping adventure!

Waiting Game!

FIRE THE LETTER

As a group, decide which letter you're going to fire. Next, try to have a conversation without using that letter. For a hard game, chose not to say a letter that's sometimes silent like "E." For an easier game, choose not to say a letter that's always easy to hear like "S." If a player accidentally uses a word that has the fired letter, they are out.

FUN FACT

*The lookout towers in
Redwood Creek Challenge
Trail are named after
mountains in California:
Mt. Lassen, Mt. Shasta
& Mt. Whitney.*

NEAT!

"A Wilderness Explorer
is a friend to all,
be it plant or
fish or tiny mole."
—RUSSELL

★ Redwood Creek Challenge Trail

CLIMBING & EXPLORING · est. 2001 · LIVELY & EXCITING

The wilderness must be explored! Pick up an Activity Map from a friendly Park Ranger and complete the six challenges to become a Senior Wilderness Explorer scout. As you complete each fun activity, you'll scratch a silver circle off the map and find an achievement badge underneath. First, you'll earn your Tracking badge by finding footprints left by Kevin—the big, colorful bird from *Up*. Next, it's on to the tire zip line to try for your Bravery badge. You'll cross a rocky cliff for the Rock Climbing badge and then climb to a lookout tower to holler into a hollow log for your Wolf Howl badge. A dark cave is where you'll discover which animal you are for your Animal Spirit badge. Last but not least, you'll find clues on animal statues to earn your Puzzle Solving badge. All done? Find a Park Ranger to get your Senior Wilderness Explorer sticker. Hurray!

HOT TIP You don't **HAVE** to use the map. Feel free to wing it and see where the wind takes you. In addition to the challenges, there are **lots** of other great places to explore in this **woodsy wonderland**.

Beaver illustration by Scott Cocking · www.SideShowDesign.com

TIME MACHINE

1916
President Wilson signs an act creating the National Park Service to protect America's parks & monuments.

2001
Time to explore! Redwood Creek Challenge Trail is an Opening Day attraction in DCA.

2003
"Brother Bear" hits theaters & Redwood Creek Challenge Trail gets a "Brother Bear" theme.

2011
Two years after "Up" hits theaters, Redwood Creek Challenge Trail gets an "Up" theme.

Which activities did you do?
- ☐ Earned my Senior Wilderness Explorer Badge
- ☐ Explored the Ranger Headquarters
- ☐ Saw a cross section of a 1,000+ year old tree
- ☐ Scrambled across swaying bridges
- ☐ Slid down a rock slide
- ☐ Strolled through the middle of a tree

EARN YOUR BADGES TODAY!

★ Grizzly River Run

Looking to cool off on a hot day? This exciting river rapids ride should do the trick! The wet-and-wild Grizzly River is the site of an abandoned mining operation. You'll board an eight-passenger round raft and travel up a 275-foot conveyer belt for an up-close view of the top of the bear-shaped Grizzly Peak mountain. You'll bob and spin in and out of tunnels through twists and turns in the river and over rushing rapids before making it back to base camp, most likely completely soaking wet!

HOT TIP
Worried about your stuff **getting wet?** This ride has its own lockers (free for up to two hours) and **Rushin' Rivers Outfitters** sells plastic ponchos.

SPY
As you walk from Grizzly River Run towards Soarin' Around the World, peek through the **free binoculars** installed beside the path.

FUN FACT

A 20-foot tall grizzly bear statue stands at the entrance to Grizzly River Run.

PHOTO OPP!

HEY KIDS
COLOR ME IN!

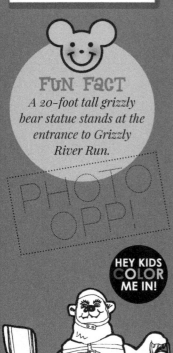

Mini Quiz!

Can you guess the name of this water wheel?
Answer on page 182.
- ☐ Eureka wheel
- ☐ Fun wheel
- ☐ Pelton wheel

TIME MACHINE

1811
The sport of river rapids rafting is born with the first recorded attempt to raft down Snake River in Wyoming.

1980
The world's first river rapids ride opens in Texas. Yeehaw!

2001
Grizzly River Run is an Opening Day attraction in DCA & has a modern, extreme sports theme.

2013
Grizzly River Run changes to a vintage California national park theme.

Scenes from Grizzly Peak Trail

Park Service truck

Remains of the mine shaft

The story goes that a coyote turned a grizzly bear to stone to watch over Grizzly Peak!

Eureka Gold & Timber building

Old mining equipment

Beautiful scenery!

FUN FACT

*A group of hang glider pilots who fly together is called a **gaggle**. Oddly enough, a group of geese is also called a gaggle but only when NOT in flight. When in flight they're called a **skein**.*

FUNNY!

MAY BE SCARY ⚠

★ Soarin' Around the World

HANG GLIDING RIDE — est. — **2001** ★ Lively & exciting ★

How would you like to fly high in the sky over some of the world's most **amazing** sights? First, you'll head into a large airplane hangar. When it's time for your flight, you'll take a seat on an awaiting **glider** and be whisked away on an incredible **journey** as your feet dangle in a gentle breeze. You'll soar through thirteen locations over astounding **natural wonders** like North America's Monument Valley, South America's Iguazu waterfalls and Switzerland's Matterhorn mountain. Your voyage will also take you past man-made **landmarks** like Australia's Sydney Opera House, China's Great Wall and Germany's Neuschwanstein Castle—the inspiration for Disneyland's Sleeping Beauty Castle. For the **grand finale** you'll fly over the happiest place on earth—the Disneyland Resort. And the **best** part of all? You don't even need a passport!

HOT TIP
This ride feels **SO** real that you just might think you can actually **smell** some of the places you're passing over—**and you can!**

SPY
As you're waiting to soar around the world, check out the **aviation history displays** around the airplane hangar.

TIME MACHINE

2001
Hang in there! Soarin' Over California is a popular Opening Day attraction in DCA.

2005
Walt Disney World in Florida gets its own version of the attraction when Soarin' opens in Epcot.

2015
Disney announces that the Soarin' attractions will get a global theme to match the new version being created for Shanghai Disneyland.

2016
Guests start soaring over the whole world instead of just California when the attractions change to Soarin' Around the World.

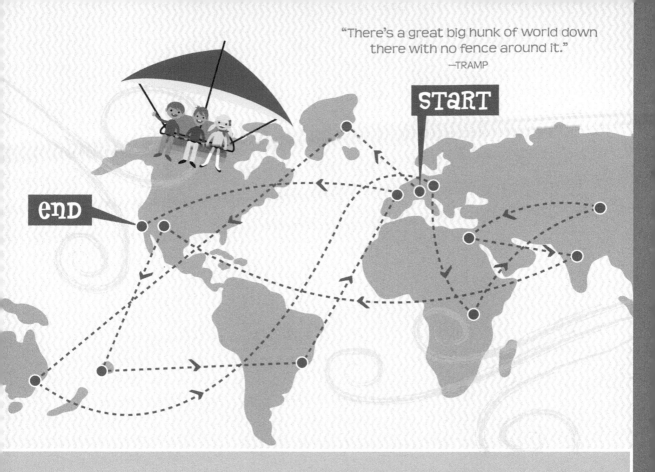

"There's a great big hunk of world down there with no fence around it."
—TRAMP

START

END

THE FATHER OF NATIONAL PARKS

Here and there around **Grizzly Peak** you'll find quotes by **John Muir.** He was a Scottish conservationist, explorer, farmer, inventor, naturalist and writer who lived from **1838-1914** and is famous for helping to **preserve land** for America's national parks. John always loved **exploring** but, when he suffered an eye injury and was confined to a dark room for **six weeks,** he vowed he'd take more time to **enjoy nature.** He travelled the world, including walking **a thousand miles** from Indiana to the Gulf of Mexico, but once he got to California he knew he was **home.** After visiting California's Sierra Nevada mountains John called them "the most **divinely beautiful** of all the mountain chains I have ever seen." John's writings about his travels and viewpoints on protecting nature had a **big impact** on the people of his time and helped show the world that natural areas need to be **preserved.**

HOT TIP The National Park Foundation has a program where **fourth grade kids**—and their entire group—can enjoy **free entry** to any park.

FUN FACT

When a forest fire is spotted, smokejumpers parachute onto the scene & set up camp with enough food & water to last them a few days. The first smokejumpers jumped on the scene in America in 1939.

AMAZING!

"Eating greens is a special treat. It makes long ears and great big feet. But it sure is awful stuff to eat. I made that last part up myself."

—THUMPER

★ Food & Drinks

SMOKEJUMPERS GRILL

The hot ticket at this quick-service hotspot is the hamburger—one of the only spots to get one in DCA. The story goes that owners Millie and Herb created the grill in honor of the Bearpaw Basin Smokejumpers. Choose to sit outside under an umbrella or inside the industrial, spacious metal hangar.

• *Chili cheese fries* • *Hamburgers* • *Milkshakes* • *Onion rings*

HOT TIP **White Water Snacks** in Disney's Grand Californian Hotel & Spa has burgers too and is within walking distance of Grizzly Peak. If you go, you will have to **exit the park** so be sure to have your ticket and get your **hand stamped** so you can get back in!

SPY Look around the **Smokejumpers Grill** to see firefighter gear, vintage Disney posters and old black-and-white photos.

Photograph by Dave DeCaro • http://davelandweb.com

BUILD YOUR BURGER!

Smokejumpers Grill has a toppings bar where you can customize your burger your way. Put a ✔ in the boxes below to create your ultimate burger.

PATTY:

☐ Beef ☐ Veggie

CONDIMENTS:

☐ BBQ sauce ☐ Ketchup ☐ Mayo ☐ Mustard
☐ Ranch dressing ☐ Thousand Island dressing

TOPPINGS:

☐ Banana peppers ☐ Jalapeno peppers ☐ Lettuce
☐ Onion ☐ Pickles ☐ Red peppers ☐ Tomato

CHOW Time!

Think you know your Disney animals? Draw a line connecting
the **character's name** to the thing they might like to **eat or drink**.
The first one's been done for you. *Answers on page 182.*

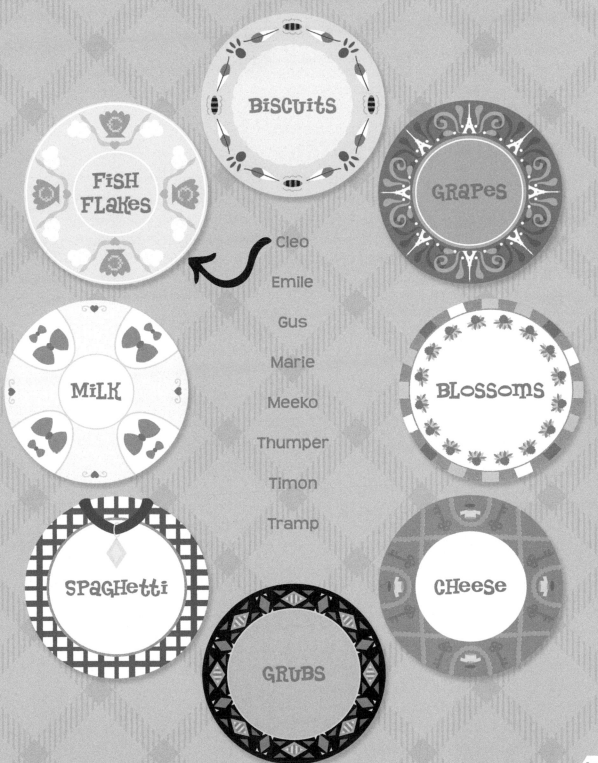

BiSCuits

FiSH FLaKes

GRaPes

Cleo

Emile

Gus

Marie

Meeko

Thumper

Timon

Tramp

MiLK

BLossoms

SPaGHetti

CHeese

GRUBs

★ Sample Souvenirs

QUARTER PRESS

There are several coin press machines located in and around DCA. Most of these machines press pennies but the one at **Rushin' River Outfitters** is the only one that presses quarters. You'll need three quarters total—one to press and two to make the machine go.

 HOT TIP Another unique coin press machine in DCA is the **dime press** at Studio Store in Hollywood Land.

SMOKEY BEAR T-SHIRT

The U.S. Forest Service manages America's national forests and grasslands. Back in 1944, they released a campaign with posters featuring Thumper, Flower and Bambi from the movie *Bambi* urging people to prevent forest fires. Later that year, the Forest Service debuted a new poster featuring a character all their own, Smokey Bear. Head to **Humphrey's Service & Supplies** to pick up a tee featuring this friendly fellow.

 SPY You can see a copy of the Forest Service's poster from 1944 featuring **Bambi and friends** across from Humphrey's Service & Supplies, near the Mt. Muir lookout tower.

DISNEY LEGEND CLOSE-UP: Retta Scott

Retta Scott grew up in Washington and moved to Los Angeles to study art. Her teacher urged her to apply for a job at the **Walt Disney Studios** and she was hired in the story department in 1938. Walt saw her work and promoted her to be an **inbetweener**—an artist who draws the frames in between the main action scenes—a job that was **rare** for women at that time. In 1941, Walt told his team that "the girl artists have the right to expect the **same chances for advancement** as men, and I honestly believe they may eventually contribute something to this business that men never would or could." After Retta was promoted to be an **animator**, her work on *Bambi* earned her the **first onscreen credit in Disney history** for a female animator. She also worked on *Fantasia*, *Dumbo* and more. Later, Retta illustrated **Disney's Cinderella Golden Book** from 1950 which is still popular today. Retta was named a **Disney Legend** in 2000.

WHERE DO I WORK?

Cast Members wear **outfits** that match the **theme** of the attraction where they work. Can you guess **which outfit** matches **which attraction**? Draw a line connecting the **outfit** to the name of the **attraction**. The first one's been done for you. *Answers on page 182.*

Goofy's Sky School

Monsters, Inc. Mike & Sulley to the Rescue

Redwood Creek Challenge Trail

The Little Mermaid ~ Ariel's Undersea Adventure

The Twilight Zone Tower of Terror

Tuck and Roll's Drive 'Em Buggies

Where would you like to work in DCA? Why?

_____

_____

_____

The real Mt. Muir in California's Sierra Nevada Mountains is named after famous conservationist John Muir.

My Trip Journal

Use this handy Trip Journal during and after your visit to DCA!

My TRiP JouRNaL-aBout My Visit to DCa

How was the weather?..

What was your favorite part of your visit?.................................

....

Was it crowded? ☐ Yes ☐ Kinda ☐ No

Did you get any souvenirs? ☐ Yes ☐ No
If yes, what did you get?

....

Draw a picture of yourself in Disney California Adventure:

My TRiP JoURNaL—aBouT My ViSiT to DCa

Which land did you like best?

☐ A Bug's Land   ☐ Buena Vista Street   ☐ Cars Land
☐ Grizzly Peak   ☐ Hollywood Land   ☐ Pacific Wharf
☐ Paradise Pier

Why was it your favorite land? ....

....

Did you see any entertainment? If so, what did you see?

....

....

What was the best ride of all? ....

....

What was the most delicious thing you ate or drank? ....

....

Did you see any characters? If so, which ones?

....

....

....

Was there anything you wanted to do but couldn't? Why?

....

....

My TRiP JouRNaL-abouT My ViSiT to DCa

Stories from your trip:

....

....

....

....

....

....

....

....

....

....

....

....

....

....

My Trip Journal-about My Visit to DCA

Stories from your trip:

....
....
....
....
....
....
....
....
....
....
....
....
....
....
....

MY TRIP JOURNAL-SCRAPBOOK

When you're visiting Disney California Adventure hold on to receipts, napkins, maps, stickers, admission tickets, PhotoPass cards, unused FastPass tickets, handouts and other flat things to tape or glue onto these pages.

MY TRIP JOURNAL-SCRAPBOOK

MY TRIP JOURNAL-SCRAPBOOK

My Trip Journal—Autographs

Characters in Disney California Adventure love to meet their fans and give autographs! Collect character autographs and stamps here.

My Trip Journal—Autographs

Write a pretend postcard to your favorite Disney character about your visit to DCA!

59 USA
59 USA
59 USA
59 USA

59 USA
59 USA
59 USA
59 USA
59 USA

59 USA
59 USA
59 USA
59 USA
59 USA

GOING TO GUIDES
www.GoingToGuides.com
Going To Disney California Adventure

59 USA

To:

Buena Vista Street illustration by Steve Willis

Super, Super-Short Stories

Visiting Disney California Adventure can be more fun when you know and love Disney characters and stories. Here are some short versions of many of the stories you'll experience and where you'll see them in the park.

a BUG'S Life

Flik is an inventor who is often getting into trouble with the other ants in his colony on Ant Island. The colony is ruled over by the Queen who has two daughters, Princess Atta and young Dot. Ant Island is bullied by a gang of grasshoppers led by Hopper who demand the ants collect food for them. Flik leaves the island to search for warrior bugs to save them. He meets a group of circus bugs (Dim, Francis, Gypsy, Heimlich, Manny, Rosie, Slim, Tuck and Roll) who have just been fired from P.T. Flea's Circus and he thinks they're the warriors he's been searching for. They agree to go with Flik, thinking he's a talent agent who can help them get new jobs. After a bird attack, Flik is inspired to build a fake bird to scare away the grasshoppers. It doesn't work but the ants rise up against the grasshoppers and refuse to work for them anymore. Princess Atta rescues Flik after he's kidnapped by Hopper—who gets his just desserts when he's snatched by a bird and fed to her chicks. As peace comes to Ant Island, the circus bugs say farewell.
ATTRACTIONS: Flik's Flyers • Francis' Ladybug Boogie • Heimlich's Chew Chew Train • It's Tough to be a Bug • Tuck and Roll's Drive 'Em Buggies

Beauty anD tHe Beast

Belle lives in a quiet village with her father Maurice who is an eccentric inventor. She loves to read and loves her father but does not love the stuck-up Gaston, even though Gaston thinks she should. Maurice gets lost in the woods and finds an enchanted castle where a young prince has been cursed and turned into a hideous beast. The Prince must earn someone's love before the last petal falls from an enchanted rose or he will be doomed to stay a beast forever. Maurice enters the castle in search of help and meets the Beast's servants who have been turned into objects as part of the curse—a candlestick (Lumiere), a clock (Cogsworth), a teapot (Mrs. Potts), a teacup (Chip) and more. The Beast is furious to find Maurice and throws him in the dungeon. Belle goes in search of her father. When she reaches the castle, she makes a deal to stay with the Beast if he'll set her father free. The Beast warns Belle to never go in the West Wing and is enraged when she does. Frightened, Belle runs into the woods and is saved from fierce wolves by the Beast, who gets injured. When Belle tends to his wounds the two become friends. Knowing she loves to read, the Beast gives Belle a library— to her delight. Belle tells the Beast she misses her father so he lets her check on him in an enchanted mirror. When she sees her father is in danger, the Beast lets her go to help him and gives her the mirror. Back in the village, Maurice  *(continues on the next page)*

177

has tried to tell the others about the Beast but no one will believe him. Gaston, hoping to force Belle to marry him, tries to get "crazy old Maurice" locked up in an insane asylum. Belle arrives in the village and proves her father is right by showing the Beast to Gaston in the mirror. Gaston gathers an angry mob to storm the castle and kill the hideous creature. After a fierce battle, Gaston falls to his death from the castle's roof and Belle reaches the dying Beast. As the last petal falls from the enchanted rose, Belle tells him "I love you." With those words, the curse is broken and the Beast and his servants become human again.
ATTRACTION: Beast's Library in Disney Animation Building

CARS

Lightning McQueen is a rookie race car with big dreams. After he's part of a three-way tie in the Piston Cup along with Chick Hicks and The King, he dreams of winning the Championship and moving up in the world by being sponsored by Dinoco instead of Rust-Eze. When Mack the Truck tows Lightning to the tiebreaker race in California, a gang of street racers (including a blue-and-green car named DJ) cause Lightning to fall off the trailer and end up in a forgotten desert town along Route 66 called Radiator Springs. After accidentally ruining the pavement, Lightning is arrested and guarded overnight by a rusty tow truck named Tow Mater. The town judge Doc Hudson agrees to lawyer Sally Carrera's plan to make Lightning repave the road and stay in Sally's Cozy Cone Motel during his sentence. During his stay, Lightning becomes friends with the townspeople including Luigi of the Casa Della Tires shop and his assistant Guido the Forklift, Ramone of Ramone's House of Body Art and his wife Flo of Flo's V8 Café, a 1960s microbus named Fillmore, a veteran military Jeep named Sarge, Red the Fire Engine, and Lizzie of Radiator Springs Curios. Before Lightning leaves Radiator Springs to go to the race in California, he learns that Doc Hudson is actually the Fabulous Hudson Hornet, a three-time winner of the Piston Cup. During the race, Lightning misses his new friends and is surprised and happy when he sees they've come to cheer him on. Though Lightning doesn't win, he shows such good sportsmanship that Dinoco offers him a sponsorship deal anyway. Lightning decides he'll stick with Rust-Eze, return to Radiator Springs and set up his headquarters there to help the town return to its former glory.
ATTRACTIONS: Luigi's Rollickin' Roadsters • Mater's Junkyard Jamboree
• Radiator Springs Racers

FINDING NEMO $ FINDING DORY

In *Finding Nemo*, a cautious clownfish named Marlin living in Australia's Great Barrier Reef is overly protective of his son Nemo. When Nemo is caught and put in an aquarium in a dentist's office, Marlin sets off to find him and bring him home. A forgetful blue tang fish named Dory joins Marlin in the search—though most of the time she doesn't remember what she's doing or what just happened! Marlin and Dory meet three sharks named Bruce, Anchor and Chum who are trying to be nicer by living by the motto "Fish are friends, not food." After escaping from a terrifying deep-sea anglerfish and beautiful but dangerous jellyfish, Marlin and Dory are shown how to ride the EAC—or East Australian Current—by Crush the Turtle and his son Squirt. Meanwhile Nemo and his new friends in the fish tank learn that Nemo is going to be given to the dentist's daughter Darla, a little girl who has already killed a fish by shaking the bag it was in. Nemo manages to escape from the fish tank and get back to the ocean where he is finally reunited with his dad.

In *Finding Dory*, Dory remembers that she was separated from her parents when she was young. With help from Crush, Marlin and Nemo, she sets off on a journey to California to try and find them. Dory is captured by workers from the Marine Life Institute and, once inside their aquarium, she learns that her parents were kept in captivity there in the past but had managed to escape. Inside the Institute, Dory meets a grumpy octopus called Hank who can camouflage himself, a whale shark named Destiny and a beluga whale named Bailey. Meanwhile Marlin and Nemo try to rescue Dory with the help of a bird named Becky. When one of the Institute's employees accidentally drops Dory into a drain, she is flushed out to the ocean and finds her parents who had been searching for her since their escape. Marlin and Nemo are put on a truck going to a different aquarium but Dory and friends manage to free them. With the whole gang reunited, everyone returns to the Great Barrier Reef.

ATTRACTION: Turtle Talk with Crush in Disney Animation Building

FROZEN

Young Princess Elsa of Arendelle and her little sister Anna love playing together and having fun with Elsa's magical ability to make snow and ice. When the girls play in the snow that Elsa creates indoors, Anna gets hurt accidentally and their parents take her to Pabbie the Troll King for help. Pabbie heals Anna and takes away her memories of Elsa's powers. Elsa's parents close down the castle and urge her to hide her uniqueness from the world. As Elsa struggles to control her powers, she stays alone in her room, shutting out the world—and Anna. Sadly, their parents die in a storm at sea and the girls grow up with only each other but always separated by Elsa's closed bedroom door. When Coronation Day arrives for Elsa to become Queen, Anna is excited that the castle will finally have visitors. She meets a handsome prince named Hans, falls in love with him and says "YES!" when he asks her to marry him—even though they just met. When Anna asks for Elsa's permission to marry Hans during the coronation celebration, Elsa becomes angry and loses control of her powers. The crowd is shocked and scared when they see what Elsa can do and she runs into the mountains where she builds an ice palace hideaway. As the town is covered in an eternal winter, Anna leaves Hans in charge of Arendelle and sets off in search of her sister. While stocking up on supplies at Wandering Oaken's Trading Post, Anna meets an ice salesman called Kristoff and his reindeer, Sven and convinces them to help her find Elsa. Along the way, the three meet Olaf the Snowman who shows them where Elsa's hideaway is. Elsa accidentally hurts Anna and creates a huge snow monster named Marshmallow to chase everyone away. Kristoff takes Anna to see the Trolls who tell them that her heart is freezing and she needs to be saved by an act of true love. Kristoff, who knows that Anna and Hans wanted to get married, rushes her to the castle so Hans can save her with true love's kiss. Meanwhile, Hans goes to the mountains in search of Anna, finds Elsa and throws her in prison. When Anna finds Hans at last, he reveals his true, cruel nature and leaves her to die. Elsa escapes her cell and runs out into the snowstorm. Olaf finds Anna and tells her that her true love is Kristoff and they rush through the snow to find him before Anna's heart freezes. When Anna sees that Hans is about to kill Elsa, she throws herself between them causing Elsa's blast to accidentally hit Anna and turn her to ice. As Elsa cries, Anna begins to thaw. The love that Anna showed by selflessly protecting her sister is the act of true love that saves her. The ice and snow melt, Hans is sent back to his own land and the sisters vow never to close down the castle again.

ATTRACTION: Frozen — Live at the Hyperion

Monsters, Inc.

The city of Monstropolis runs on the power in the screams of terrified children. The monsters who work at Monsters, Inc. go through kids' bedroom doors on the Scare Floor, frighten them and collect their screams. Monsters Mike Wazowski and James P. Sullivan (nicknamed "Sulley") work together as a team. Sulley is the company's top scarer and Mike is his assistant while supervisor Roz is "always watching." A sly monster named Randall, who can make himself invisible by changing his skin to match his surroundings, leaves a door activated on the Scare Floor and a little girl named Boo enters the factory. The citizens of Monstropolis are terrified of human children and the toxic germs they think they carry. Sulley takes Boo with him to get help from Mike who is on a fancy date with snake-haired Celia to celebrate her birthday at Harryhausen's Sushi Restaurant. When the monsters realize the human is near, panic breaks out and rumors start to fly. The yellow-suited Child Detection Agency (CDA) scour the city to find the girl and contain the human germs. Sulley realizes that Boo isn't dangerous and that her laughter is more powerful than her screams. After making Boo a monster disguise, Mike and Sulley return to Monsters, Inc. to try to get her back home but they discover that Randall has built a Scream Extractor machine. When Mike and Sulley tell Randall's evil plans to Monsters, Inc. chairman Henry J. Waternoose, he reveals that he and Randall are in cahoots, exiles Mike and Sulley to the Himalayas and takes Boo. Stranded in the snowy wasteland, they are helped by a friendly Yeti who offers them yellow, lemon-flavored snow cones. After getting back to Monstropolis, Sulley rescues Boo and Mike rejoins his friend to help. Randall chases the trio through the Door Vault where the kids' bedrooms doors are stored. Mike and Sulley manage to send Randall through a door where he's mistaken for an alligator and hit with a shovel. After the CDA arrests Waternoose, Roz reveals that she is the leader of the Agency and has been working undercover at Monsters, Inc. After Sulley finally gets Boo back home, he becomes the new head of the company and changes the whole operation so Monstropolis is powered by children's laughter instead of screams.

ATTRACTION: Monsters, Inc. Mike & Sulley to the Rescue

The Little Mermaid

Ariel the Mermaid lives under the sea with her father King Triton and her six sisters but daydreams of living on land. She's friends with Flounder the Fish, Sebastian the Crab and Scuttle the Seagull who she chats with about her collection of objects from the human world. When King Triton sees her collection, he is furious and orders her to stop daydreaming. Ariel returns to the surface anyway and falls in love with the handsome Prince Eric as he celebrates his birthday on his boat. During a terrible storm, Eric is tossed overboard and Ariel rescues him from drowning. As she holds him on the beach, she sings to him in her angelic voice. When he wakes up, she's gone and he vows to find her. Yearning for Eric, Ariel visits Ursula the Sea Witch who captures Ariel's voice in a nautilus shell and uses her magic to give her legs instead of her mermaid tail. Ursula warns Ariel that she only has three days to get Eric to kiss her or Ariel's voice—and soul—will be hers forever. Wobbling on her new legs, Ariel walks onto the beach and wraps herself in an old sail. Eric and his dog Max find her and take her back to his castle. Eric wonders if she was the mysterious girl who saved him but thinks he must be mistaken when he learns she can't speak. As the two grow closer, they share a romantic boat ride and Eric leans in to kiss Ariel. Ursula's evil eels Flotsam and Jetsam tip over the boat to prevent the kiss and Ursula realizes Ariel is getting too close to winning Eric's heart. Disguising herself as a beautiful woman named Vanessa, Ursula uses Ariel's voice and her magic to trick Eric into agreeing to marry her. At last Ariel gets her voice back and Eric wakes from his spell to realize she's the girl he's been searching for. After a fierce battle between Ursula, who has

returned to her Sea Witch form, and King Triton, Ursula is defeated. When King Triton sees how much Ariel truly loves Eric, he uses his power to turn her into a human forever.
ATTRACTION: The Little Mermaid ~ Ariel's Undersea Adventure

Toy Story 1, 2 & 3

In *Toy Story*, Sheriff Woody, Mr. Potato Head, Hamm the Piggy Bank, Rex the Tyrannosaurus Rex, Slinky Dog, Bo Peep and the rest of the toys belong to a little boy named Andy and come to life when humans aren't around. The toys welcome a new spaceman action figure called Buzz Lightyear to Andy's Room but soon discover he thinks he's a real Space Ranger and doesn't know he's a toy! When Buzz ends up next door at Sid's house, he sees a commercial for a Buzz Lightyear action figure and is depressed to realize that he's just a toy. Woody convinces him being a toy is actually a good thing and together they escape and make it back home.

In *Toy Story 2,* Woody is taken by a vintage toy collector and finds out there used to be a TV show about him called *Woody's Roundup* which also starred Jessie the Cowgirl and Bullseye the Horse. Woody, Jessie and Bullseye become friends and escape before they can be sent to a toy museum. When Buzz and some of the other toys end up in a toy store, they encounter an evil Emporer Zurg toy who tries to destroy Buzz but is defeated.

In *Toy Story 3,* Woody, Buzz and some of the other toys end up being donated to a day-care center which is run by a toy bear tyrant named Lotso. After making their escape, Woody and his friends find a home with a little girl named Bonnie and her toys including Buttercup the Unicorn and Trixie the Triceratops.
ATTRACTION: Toy Story Midway Mania

UP

Back in the good old days, Carl Fredricksen had his beloved Ellie by his side. The two had met as children and realized they were both fans of the famous explorer Charles Muntz. Ellie gives Carl a pin made from a grape soda bottlecap and tells him she wants to fix up an abandoned house in their neighborhood and move it to a cliff in Paradise Falls—an exotic faraway location where Muntz says he discovered the skeleton of a giant exotic bird. When Carl and Ellie get married, Ellie opens a zoo where Carl sells balloons. They buy the abandoned house, fix it up and dream of starting a family. When things don't work out, they decide to save their money to go to Paradise Falls but can never manage to make it there. In their old age Carl finally plans the trip but Ellie becomes sick and passes away. Now an old man, the neighborhood around Carl's house is changing but he stubbornly refuses to move. After accidentally hurting a construction worker, Carl is ordered by a judge to move to a retirement home. Determined to keep his promise to Ellie, Carl attaches thousands of helium balloons to his house to float it to Paradise Falls. A Wilderness Explorer scout named Russell comes to his house to try to earn a merit badge but Carl sends him away. When the house begins to lift into the air, Carl discovers Russell is on the porch and brings him inside to safety. The house lands right across from Paradise Falls, and Carl and Russell try to get the house in the right spot before the balloons deflate. They meet a giant exotic bird who Russell names Kevin. After meeting a dog named Dug and a pack of agressive dogs (who can all talk thanks to a special collar), the group is taken to meet the dogs' master who turns out to be Charles Muntz. Muntz tells Carl and Russell that he's spent his life looking for the giant bird so he could prove to the world that it really exists and he's not crazy. Russell realizes he's talking about Kevin. After Carl and Russell save Kevin from Muntz's evil plans, they return home where Carl presents Russell with his final merit badge—the grape soda bottlecap that Ellie had given to him.
ATTRACTION: Redwood Creek Challenge Trail

Game Answers

PAGE 24—Golden State Pop Quiz!
(1) Grizzly Bear (2) California Quail (3) Sacramento (4) California Poppy (5) Eureka!

PAGE 26—Phony Baloney!
Daisy Duck's Depot

PAGE 28—Shoe Shopping!
Alice, Mickey Mouse, Honey Lemon, Woody, Tinker Bell, Jafar, Cinderella, Anna

PAGE 29—Road Trip!
Clockwise from top left: New Mexico, Kansas, Arizona, Illinois, Oklahoma, Missouri, California, Texas
BONUS QUESTION:
California > Arizona > New Mexico > Texas > Oklahoma > Kansas > Missouri > Illinois

PAGE 33—Guess the DisneyBound!
Mickey Mouse, Ariel, Robin Hood, Daisy Duck, Smee
BONUS QUESTION:
Dr. Facilier

PAGE 45—Character Color Schemes!
Row 1: Chip, Ariel, Mickey Mouse, Donald Duck
Row 2: Goofy, Belle, Daisy Duck, Peter Pan
Row 3: Pluto, Sulley, Minnie Mouse, Woody
Row 4: Nemo, Judy Hopps, Russell, Anna

PAGE 53—Say What? Kid Edition!
Anna "The sky's awake so I'm awake."
Baby Dory "I suffer from short term remembery loss."
Hiro Hamada "Can I try? I have a robot. I built it myself."
Michael Darling "He flewed!"
Mowgli "I'll do anything to stay in the jungle!"
Pete "Are you going to eat me?"
Pinocchio "But father, I'm alive. See?"
Riley "I know you don't want me to, but I miss home."

PAGE 68—Mini Quiz!
Dan Walker

PAGE 69—Who Shops Where?
Carl Fredricksen = House Balloons; Edna = A La Mode Eyewear; Elsa = Gloves of Arendelle; Goofy = The Hat Shoppe; Mickey Mouse = The Shorts Emporium; Mike Wazowski = Harryhausen's Take-Out; The Beast = Belle Jars; Ursula = Undersea Bottles; Woody = Snake In My Boot Boots

PAGE 77—Speaking Pig Latin!
"I can't wait to ride Monsters, Inc. Mike and Sulley to the Rescue!"

PAGE 85—Award Winners!
"A Whole New World" = *Aladdin;* "Beauty and the Beast" = *Beauty and the Beast;* "Can You Feel the Love Tonight" = *The Lion King;* "Chim Chim Cher-ee" = *Mary Poppins;* "Colors of the Wind" = *Pocahontas;* "If I Didn't Have You" = *Monsters, Inc.;* "Let It Go" = *Frozen;* "Under the Sea" = *The Little Mermaid;* "When You Wish Upon a Star" = *Pinocchio;* "You'll Be in My Heart" = *Tarzan*

PAGE 89—Costume Call!
White Rabbit, Pinocchio, Snow White's Prince, Flynn Rider, Goofy, Fear, Aladdin, Woody, Judy Hopps

PAGE 101—Say What? Disney•Pixar Edition!

Carl Fredricksen "So long, boys! I'll send you a postcard from Paradise Falls!"
Dug "I was hiding under your porch because I love you."
Edna Mode "No capes!"
Francis "So, bein' a ladybug automatically makes me a girl. Is that it, flyboy?"
Mrs. Potato Head "I'm packing you an extra pair of shoes and your angry eyes—just in case."
Roz "Your stunned silence is very reassuring."
Wreck-It Ralph "I am bad and that's good. I will never be good and that's not bad."

PAGE 107—Cars Name Scrambles!

Lightning McQueen, Mater, Doc Hudson, Sally Carrera, Ramone, Luigi, Chick Hicks, Fillmore, Lizzie, Guido

PAGE 113—Motorama Girls Match-Up!

Flo = "She's Fin-Tastic!"; Laverne = "Va-Va-Vroom!"; Rhonda = "What a Creampuff!"; Sheila = "Sassy & Classy!"

PAGE 115—Mini Quiz!

Willys MB

PAGE 115—Bumper Sticker Bonanza!

Row 1: Woody, Ariel, Grumpy
Row 2: Carl Fredricksen, Captain Hook, Fa Zhou
Row 3: Cruella de Ville, Belle, Nick Wilde

PAGE 123—Mini Quiz!

Victorian

PAGE 128—Mini Quiz!

Disneyland's Matterhorn Bobsleds

PAGE 146—Hurry, Hurry, Hurry, Step Right Up!

Cotton candy

PAGE 137—Goofy Fun!

Lesson 1: How to Takeoff
Lesson 2: How to Fly
Lesson 3: How to Turn
Lesson 4: How to Nosedive
Lesson 5: How to Land

PAGE 147—Super Sidekicks!

Ariel = Flounder; Bambi = Thumper; Kristoff = Sven; Mickey Mouse = Pluto; Mowgli = Baloo; Mulan = Mushu; Peter Pan = Tinker Bell; Pocahontas = Flit; Rapunzel = Pascal; Zeus = Hermes

PAGE 154—Mini Quiz!

Pelton wheel

PAGE 159—Chow Time!

Cleo = Fish flakes; Emile = Grapes; Gus = Cheese; Marie = Milk; Meeko = Biscuits; Thumper = Blossoms; Timon = Grubs; Tramp = Spaghetti

PAGE 161—Where Do I Work?

Clockwise from top left:
The Twilight Zone Tower of Terror
Tuck and Roll's Drive 'Em Buggies
Goofy's Sky School
The Little Mermaid ~ Ariel's Undersea Adventure
Monsters, Inc. Mike & Sulley to the Rescue
Redwood Creek Challenge Trail

DID YOU HAVE FUN PLAYING THE GAMES? MEOW-VELOUS!

Heartfelt Thanks

During high school and college, I worked in the children's section at the fabulous Coronado Public Library daydreaming of creating my own book someday. It took me almost *eight years* (off and on—mostly off) to create *Going To Disneyland: A Guide for Kids & Kids at Heart* and it has been an absolute thrill to hear from readers, friends and family about how much they love the book. What a feeling!

Working on this book was a total blast! Of course, I couldn't do it alone and there are so many people to thank so I'll start the Thanking Party off by thanking my wonderful parents for giving me feedback on my ideas and even helping to proofread. If you spot any typos, please send me an email and I'll forward it to my folks! Next, I have to thank my squad—the hubs and sons Edward and Clark. You guys are Le Best and were really there for me near the end of this project when things got "cray cray". ;)

Thank you to the dear friends who helped me research, brainstorm, fact check and more—especially my beloved brother (and friend) THE Steve Willis, the simply superb Julie Siegel, the sharp-as-a-tack Kim Carpenter, the utterly fabulous Stacie Smith and the one-and-only Toni Morris. Toni and I actually spent an entire day combing DCA with a notepad and a camera, peeking into every nook and cranny, asking questions and not going on one single ride. It was weird—but fun because I was with my oldest friend. I also want to thank Summer Albin. She didn't help me with this guide in any way but she got so excited when I thanked her in my first one that I've just got to do it again! Summer's son Elliott DID help though so thank you Elliott for lending a hand—well, *both* hands—with the Swat the Bug game photos.

Huge thanks go to all of the contributing artists for sharing their amazing illustrations and photos. You guys are so talented and each one of you inspires me so much with your fabulous work. Thank you especially to the Going To Guides Official Photographer Dave DeCaro who was just INCREDIBLE about getting me the photos I needed. New to this book are contributions of a different sort including photos from DisneyBounders Tisha, little Sophie, the Foster-Riley family and DisneyBound founder Leslie Kay. Thank you all for sharing your photos with me and being a part of the fun!

Helping for the first time are Magic Kingdom Mamas. Not only did these ladies provide their wonderful tips (see page 52), they helped me so-o-o-o many times when I had details that I needed to verify. I can't imagine where I would have been without you two, seriously!

Thank you to Orchard Hill Press for being the best publisher ever, and to my unbelievably knowledgeable editor Hugh Allison. Hugh has an uncanny ability to point out things I would have never thought of in a million years and I can't even imagine how I could have created this book without him. Thanks also to Hugh's network of experts—Alison Blanchard, VJ Hicks, Sheraz Javed, David Koenig, Linda Large, Alex Villa, and Hugh's mum Sylvia Allison.

Above all, I want to thank **YOU** for buying this book! I hope you enjoy it and that you'll let me know what you think via email, snail mail, social media, carrier pigeon, skywriting... well, you get the idea. Let's keep in touch!

xoxo,
Shannon

Going To Guides • PO Box 217 • Lafayette, CA 94549
www.GoingToGuides.com
Instagram, Facebook and Twitter: @GoingToGuides

Contributor Credits

Most photos without rounded corners or frames are courtesy of the Going To Guides Official Photographer Dave DeCaro. To see more of Dave's work, visit http://davelandweb.com

Throughout this book, all photos and illustrations without a credit are by author Shannon W. Laskey.

Illustrations by contributing artists are given a credit on the page on which they appear and are listed below as well. Many images are available for purchase as fine art prints or on other products. Support your favorite artists —and be sure to tell them you saw them here!

CONTRIBUTORS:

Aaron Albarran
Ice Cream Bars, pg. 15 & 55
Groot, pg. 83
Up House, pg. 101
Minnie Bow Patch, pg. 134
Carl, pg. 146
To see more of Aaron's work, visit www.manandthemouse.com

Dan Bakst
Suitcase, pg. 13
Waffle, pg. 23
Tsum Tsum Toys, pg. 49
To see more of Dan's work, visit www.danbakst.com

Morgane Barret
White Rabbit, pg. 43
Anna & Elsa, pg. 81
To see more of Morgane's work, visit www.etsy.com/fr/shop/LeroiFrankyBoutique

Scott Cocking
Beaver, pg. 152
Redwood Creek Fun, pg. 153
Bear, pg. 154
To see more of Scott's work, visit www.SideShowDesign.com

J. Shari Ewing
Red Car Trolley, pg. 63
Cars Land, pg. 113
To see more of Shari's work, visit www.jshariewingart.com

Lindsay Gibson
Little Green Man, pg. 30
Donald, pg. 44
Squishy, pg. 74
Monsters, Inc., pg. 77
Figaro, pg. 183
To see more of Lindsay's work, visit www.etsy.com/shop/emandsprout

Michalina Grzegorz
Ariel & Her Sisters, pg. 30
Little Anna, pg. 53
Jumpin' Jellyfish, pg. 138
To see more of Michalina's work, visit www.etsy.com/shop/sketchesofmichelle

Gabrielle Jean
Mickey's Fun Wheel, pg. 134
To see more of Gabrielle's work, visit www.littlemoondance.storenvy.com

Marisa Lerin
Round date stamps, various pages
To see more of Marisa's work, visit www.pixelscrapper.com

Magic Kingdom Mamas
Julie Mooney and Emily Sims
Top 5 Tips for Visiting with Littles, pg. 52
To learn more about Magic Kingdom Mamas, visit @magic_kingdom_mamas on Facebook and Instagram or www.mkmamas.com

Lisa Penney
The Little Mermaid, pg. 141
To see more of Lisa's work, visit www.lisapenney.com

Emma Terry
Walt Disney Portrait, pg. 27
To see more of Emma's work, visit www.emmaterry.bigcartel.com

Kirsten Ulve
Alice in Wonderland, pg. 6
Jellyfish, pg. 143
To see more of Kirsten's work, visit www.KirstenUlve.com

W. Jason Weesner
Golden Zephyr, pg. 139

Steve Willis
Buena Vista Street, pg. 176

Index

The Balloons-Over-DCA Game!

GETTING STARTED

You'll need 14 coins. They do not all have to be the same type of coin. Place them on every balloon except the Mickey balloon to begin. As you play new games, choose different balloons to be the one without a coin at the beginning.

HOW TO PLAY

Pick up the coin of your choice & jump over another coin to land on an empty balloon. You may jump horizontally OR diagonally. Remove the coin you jumped over & continue until you have no jumps left. If you end up with 4 or more coins, keep practicing. If you have 2–3 coins left, that's not too shabby. If you get down to only 1 coin, you are an absolute genus!

CPSIA information can be obtained
at www.ICGtesting.com
Printed in the USA
FSOW04n2140101117
40841FS